THE REPUBLIC BASEBALL LEAGUE

OTHER BOOKS WRITTEN BY JONATHAN A. FINK

The Music Gods are Real

The Music Gods are Real - Vol. 1: The Road to the Show
The Music Gods are Real - Vol. 2: The Religion of Music
The Music Gods are Real - Vol. 3: The Winter Tour

The Baseball Gods are Real

The Baseball Gods are Real - Vol. 1: A True Story about Baseball and Spirituality
The Baseball Gods are Real - Vol. 2: The Road to the Show
The Baseball Gods are Real - Vol. 3: The Religion of Baseball

The Football Gods are Real

The Football Gods are Real - Vol. 1: The Religion of Football

The REPUBLIC BASEBALL LEAGUE

JONATHAN FINK

author of *The Baseball Gods Are Real*

The Republic Baseball League

A Novel by Jonathan A. Fink

Polo Grounds Publishing LLC

Credit and thank you to Meg Schader for editing.

Credit and thank you to Meg Reid for book cover design and book layout.

Credit and thank you to Leslie Banks for book cover photograph.

Credit and thank you to Abi Laksono for the Polo Grounds Publishing logo.

Credit and thank you to Kim Watson for biography photo.

A very special credit and thank you to my parents, Beth and Jeff Fink, for their editing, advice, and guidance related to this publication and for their unconditional love and support throughout my life.

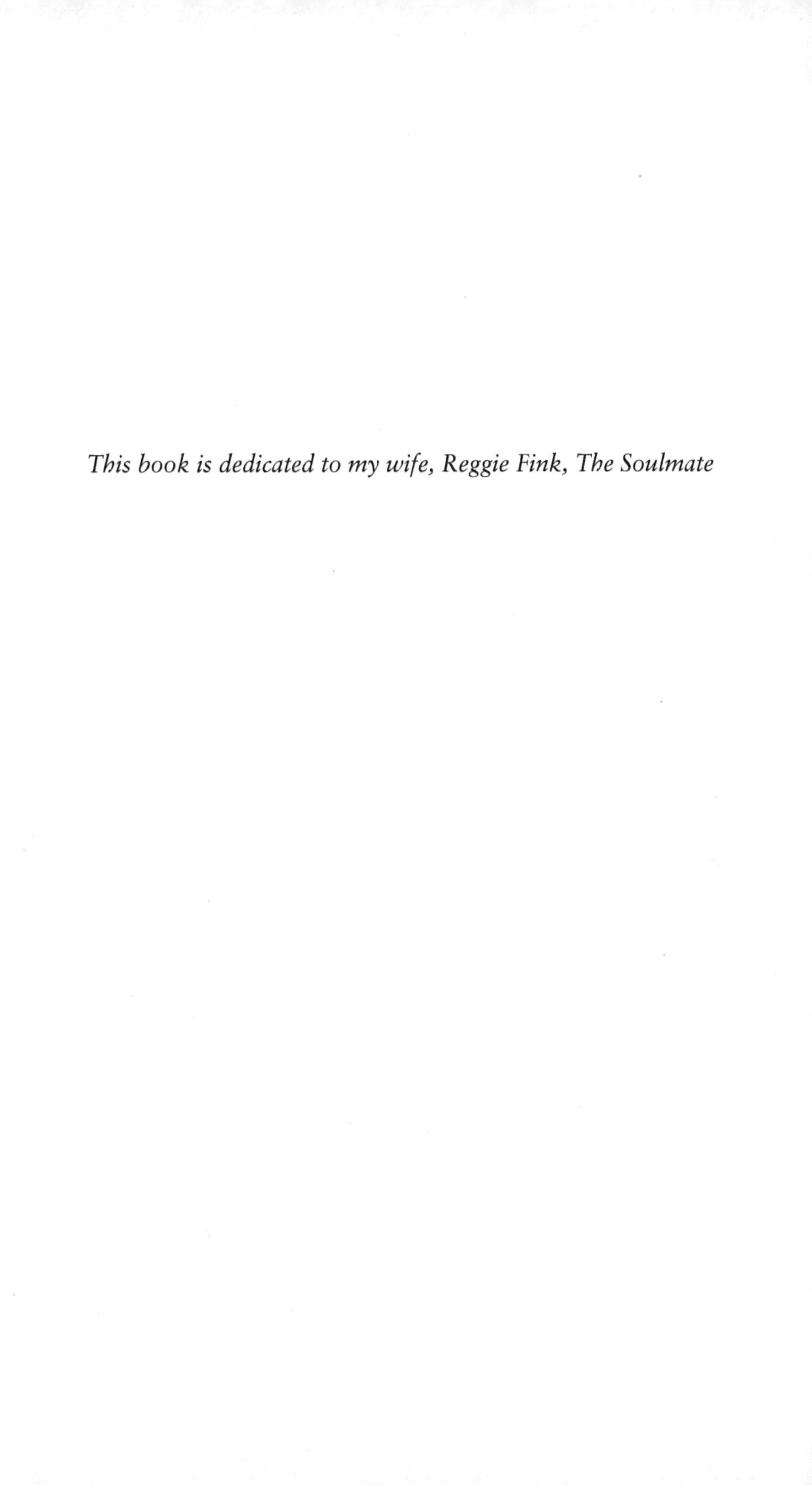

This book is dedicated to my wife, Reggie Fink, The Soulmate

TABLE OF CONTENTS

CHAPTER ONE

The Barber Shop

THE BASEBALL CARD STORE KNOWN AS "THE BARBER Shop" is located across the street from the Negro Leagues Baseball Museum on the corner of 18th and Vine Street in the historic downtown area of Kansas City. The store got its name back in 1924, during the first golden age of baseball, because the storefront used to be an authentic, old school barber shop. Through the roaring 1920s with its booming American economy, and even throughout the hard times of the Great Depression in the 1930s, The Barber Shop, with its deep roots of family and tradition, thrived and remained profitable. The store also served as the mecca of the neighborhood. For more than five decades, The Barber Shop was the place where locals would gather, talk, gossip, and debate world news and events.

The Barber Shop had an interesting history. In 1923, a baseball stadium known as Muehlebach Field was built in downtown Kansas City, just a stone's throw from the Jazz District near 18th and Vine. A year later, four brothers from Lawrence, Kansas, agreed to go into business together. Moe Franklin and his baseball obsessed older brothers pooled their life savings and agreed to open a barber shop somewhere close to the new baseball stadium. After doing some research, the Franklin brothers realized that they did not have enough money to get their new business venture off the ground. So, they agreed to seek a bank loan.

A week later, Moe Franklin sat side by side with his brothers in front of a banker named Ira Gold at First Liberty Republic Bank. Moe told Mr. Gold his family history and explained in detail how his great grandparents escaped from a slave plantation in Missouri. For days without food or water, they wandered the countryside of rolling hills and forests until they found their way to the Kansas state line, where freedom awaited them.

Gold, a short, stocky young man in his late 20s, was wearing a dark blue pinstriped suit and a powder blue bow tie. He paused, breathed deeply, removed his reading glasses, and put down his pen. He decided to tell the Franklin brothers his family story about how they arrived in Kansas City. Gold explained that his parents survived the Russian Pogroms in the early 1900s. They escaped from their village in southwestern Russia, now known as Odessa, Ukraine, by hiding deep under a pile of hay on the back of a flatbed truck. Then, by the grace of God, they managed to board a ship headed to Ellis Island, New York, in the United States of America. After a long and difficult journey across the Atlantic Ocean, the ship was not permitted to dock at Ellis Island. Much to his parents' disappointment, the ship got detoured and was directed to continue its long journey to the port of New Orleans.

It was August when the ship finally arrived and the Louisiana weather was extremely hot and humid, way too hot for his parents. So, with the little money they had left, they got on the first train they could and headed north. They rode that train to the end of the line and got off at the last stop. The last stop was central station in Kansas City, Missouri.

Gold explained that his parents initially struggled to make ends meet in their new country. But they were bright, hard-working, and realized that starting their own business would be a good idea. To do so, they sought a bank loan. Gold said, "Care to guess which bank was willing to lend my immigrant parents startup money? It was this bank, First Liberty Republic Bank. Years later, after I became the first person in my family to graduate from college, I applied for a job at the bank and they hired me."

Gold revealed that after his parents secured that small business bank loan, they opened a food stand at Kansas City Farmer's Market. His parents committed themselves to the business and prayed to God for their new venture to be a success. Their prayers were answered and profits accumulated every year. The business was so successful that over the next decade, they saved enough money to start another business, a fruit distribution enterprise. That venture was also successful and increased in size over the years to become the largest fruit distributor in the Midwest. At that point, Gold opened the top draw of his desk, took out an envelope, and handed a small business loan check to Moe Franklin. Gold shook Moe's hand and said, "Congratulations Mr. Franklin. Go now and fulfill your own American dream."

The Franklin brothers immediately put the bank loan to work and their barber shop opened a few months later on April 1, 1924, just in time for the baseball season to begin. The shop was an instant success, just as the Franklin brothers, and Mr. Gold, had hoped. Always busy with locals, there would be a long line of customers waiting for a haircut on days when there was a home game at the ballpark. As the years, and even decades, went by, professional baseball teams came and went, but the barber shop remained the same neighborhood landmark it had been since the day the brothers opened for business.

However, circumstances change and nothing lasts forever. That was the case for the good times and profits at The Barber Shop. In 1968, the Kansas City Athletics, the local Major League Baseball franchise, relocated to Oakland, California. As a result, Kansas City's downtown ballpark, then known as Municipal Stadium, was left without a tenant. The officials of Kansas City were unable to attract another professional baseball team to the city and Municipal Stadium was officially closed in 1972. The local economy suffered. Economic conditions in downtown Kansas City got even worse in 1976 when Municipal Stadium was demolished.

Inevitably, the economy of Kansas City's downtown community went into a dramatic tailspin. In the years that followed, many businesses failed and families moved out of the city and headed for the suburbs, such as Lee's Summit in Missouri and Overland Park in Kansas. The Jazz District, once thriving seven nights a week with large crowds and live music, was a shadow of its former self. The local streets that previously surrounded the baseball stadium were now lined with boarded-up storefronts and littered with uncollected bags of trash. While the local newspapers described the state of the downtown Kansas City economy as a recession, for The Barber Shop it felt more like a great depression. Sadly, in 1978, The Barber Shop closed its door and went out of business.

Four decades later in 2018, The Barber Shop reincarnated. Moe Franklin's grandson, also named Moe, who looked like comedian Kevin Hart, raised $10,000 on a GoFundMe page to open a baseball card shop on the corner of 18th and Vine Street in downtown Kansas City, the exact location where the Franklin brothers had their original barber shop. Although the store would sell baseball cards and memorabilia, not haircuts and shaves, grandson Moe named his baseball card store The Barber Shop to pay homage to his grandfather.

Grandson Moe graced the walls of the baseball card shop with photos of baseball legends including Satchel Paige, Oscar Charleston, and Buck O'Neil. Behind the counter, above an old-fashioned Coca-Cola refrigerator holding glass bottles of Coke, between a photo of Josh Gibson and James "Cool Papa" Bell, was a framed photograph of Moe's grandfather, Moe Franklin Sr. Fittingly, on April 1, 2018, exactly 94 years later to the day, Moe's baseball card store, The Barber Shop, opened for business.

Most everyday customers spent their time in the front of the store perusing The Barber Shop's incredible collection of vintage baseball cards. The locals from the neighborhood, however, typically gathered in the back room of the store to talk, gossip, and debate world news and events, just like folks did in the old days. Most of the time the discussions revolved around the game of baseball. One of the locals who spent a good deal of his spare time in the back room of The Barber Shop was a college professor named Kevin Dempsey.

CHAPTER TWO

The College Professor

KEVIN DEMPSEY WAS BORN IN 1967 AND GREW UP ON a small farm northeast of Wichita. His father loved baseball and instilled in him his passion for the game. They regularly played catch in their backyard and, during Dempsey's elementary school years, they often made the three-hour drive to Kansas City where Municipal Stadium used to be so that his dad could reminisce about "the good old days." During these visits, they frequently walked the downtown streets and strolled around the Jazz District to listen to the music blasting out of the local bars and music joints. A few times, they even got haircuts at The Barber Shop. Some of Dempsey's most cherished childhood memories were made walking these city blocks with his dad. For his father, this neighborhood was sacred ground.

Dempsey became a fantastic baseball player and was the star of the Wichita East High School team. During his senior year, he was heavily recruited by several colleges with prestigious Division 1 baseball programs, including Texas Christian University, University of Arkansas, and University of Oklahoma. Dempsey, also an excellent student who graduated high school with honors, became a local hero when he decided to stay close to home and the family farm to play ball for Wichita State University.

Dempsey made a name for himself on the baseball diamond playing shortstop for the Shockers and he led the team to several NCAA tournaments and College World Series appearances during the late 1980s. He also made a name for himself as a scholar athlete at WSU, earning a bachelor of arts degree in economics, graduating cum laude. Dempsey's achievements at WSU didn't end there. In his freshman year, he met a local girl named Sarah, a bright, beautiful Political Science major, and they dated throughout college. Immediately after graduation, they got married.

Many talented college baseball players have hopes and dreams of playing in the major leagues. Dempsey shared this dream as a youngster, but knew it was a long shot for him. He also knew that he and Sarah wanted something even more. He wanted to go to graduate school and get a master's degree in economics and then become a college professor. Sarah, who resembled actress Reece Witherspoon, wanted to go to law school and become an attorney. Dempsey's ultimate goal was to earn a PhD in economics. Having clearly defined objectives for their future, they packed their bags and moved from Wichita to Lawrence to pursue their respective graduate degrees.

Dempsey applied to the Master's in Economics program

at the University of Kansas and Sarah applied to the University of Kansas School of Law. With excellent academic credentials, both were accepted. Over the next three years, Dempsey earned his master's degree and Sarah graduated with a law degree. Both did well in graduate school and had no trouble finding employment after graduation, Dempsey as an associate college professor of economics at University of Missouri-Kansas City and Sarah at one of Kansas City's largest law firms.

Over the next two decades, the Dempsey's built a life together. They had two children, bought a house in Mission Hills, Kansas, and pursued their careers. Dempsey became a full-time professor of economics and his classes were almost always oversubscribed by students wanting to learn his curriculum. Sarah spent several years at the law firm before branching out to start her own boutique firm with a few other attorneys who left with her. They also became very involved in their community. Dempsey, who still loved baseball as much as an adult as he did as a kid, coached his boys in Little League and in youth baseball tournaments after that. As a true baseball fanatic, he continued to coach and instruct neighborhood kids on the ballfields even after his own boys went off to college. He and Sarah were active at their church and could always be counted on to do volunteer work. Dempsey did have one regret. His busy life during these years did not permit him to pursue his goal of earning his PhD. But that would change.

In 2018, the Kansas City Urban Youth Baseball Academy, the brainchild of Dayton Moore when he was the General Manager of the Kansas City Royals, opened for business on East 17th Terrace, not far from the Negro Leagues Baseball Museum and the intersection of 18th and Vine. It was built to help inner-city kids find a place to play baseball and improve their skills. As soon as the baseball academy started advertising to fill staff positions, Dempsey volunteered to be a baseball coach and drove into the city many afternoons to do so.

The Barber Shop, Moe Franklin's baseball card store, was the first new business to open after the baseball academy. Since Dempsey was already in the neighborhood, he was the first customer to walk into the store on its opening day. Dempsey returned to the store most days that he was in town, and every time he stepped inside, fond memories of his childhood with his dad resurfaced. He felt like a kid again. He also cherished these visits because he loved baseball and still enjoyed collecting baseball cards, a hobby he started as a teenager.

Dempsey's wife Sarah, now the managing partner of her boutique law firm, was always busy making sure that it ran smoothly, and it did. As a result, Dempsey had a lot of alone time on his hands and he used it wisely. Now in his 50s, sporting a college professor look, handsome with dirty blonde hair, blue eyes, and a bushy beard, he taught college and graduate level economics courses at University of Missouri-Kansas City, he coached and hit ground balls to the local kids on the baseball fields at the Kansas City Urban Youth Baseball Academy, and he spent time reminiscing and talking baseball in the back room of The Barber Shop.

Despite his busy schedule, Dempsey always found time

to think about and research ideas for his thesis to earn his PhD in economics. He spent countless hours in the university library during the week and on the weekends. Most of this time, he was on the third floor near the microfiche machines, nestled in at a desk surrounded by large stacks of books dealing with politics, economics, and the business of baseball. For months now, Dempsey had been thinking of a compelling PhD thesis but had been unable to convince Dean McGregor, the chairman of the economics department at the university, that the subject matter he had hoped to focus on was PhD dissertation worthy.

The current situation was disappointing to Dempsey. He knew that a PhD, also known as a doctorate, was the most advanced degree he could earn in his academic discipline. He would have to produce original research that expanded the boundaries of knowledge on a specific topic, normally in the form of a thesis and an oral dissertation. It would have to be worthy of publication in a peer-reviewed journal. He also knew that before he could begin his dissertation project in earnest, his subject matter would have to be approved by Dean McGregor and, after its completion, he would have to defend his work against experts in the field.

Unfortunately, Dempsey, with no new ideas to propose, sensed that today's meeting with Dean McGregor would probably be unproductive, much shorter, and possibly far worse than his previous two sessions when all of his thesis proposals were rejected. He was right. Dean McGregor, a stern, confident, well-dressed academic in his late 60s, who looked like a sinister villain right out of a James Bond movie, was sitting behind the large desk in his office. Dempsey knocked, walked in and sat down in the chair in front of the desk. He looked Dean McGregor in the eyes, and said, "I got nothing new. I still think my previous ideas are solid PhD material." The Dean looked straight back at Dempsey and replied, "Well then, this meeting is adjourned." Dempsey got up out of his chair, extended his hand to shake Dean McGregor's, and said, "Thanks for your time." McGregor did not shake Dempsey's hand. Instead, responded coldly, with a sharp tongue, "Speaking of time, mine is valuable. So please don't waste it again. This was our third meeting. Since you love baseball so much, consider this strike three and you're out. This meeting is over."

Dejected, Dempsey drove from the university campus directly to The Barber Shop. When he arrived, he walked into the back room and saw Moe Franklin sitting around a bridge table playing "Baseball Card Poker" with three old timers, Henry, Frank, and Bobby. In baseball card poker, every player received a pack of baseball cards. Then the players traded cards with each other hoping to make one of several winning hands. For example, "Four of a Kind" would be four players on the same baseball team. A "Full House" would be one card of a ballplayer from five different teams in the same division. A "Royal Flush" would be a hand of five cards of players on the Kansas City Royals. If no player had a winning hand, each received another pack of baseball cards and trading continued.

When it came to baseball memorabilia at The Barber Shop, the back room was just as jam packed as the front of the store. The walls were adorned with colorful baseball pennants of teams from the past, including the Homestead

Grays, the St. Louis Stars, the Pittsburgh Crawfords, and the Newark Eagles. Photos of dozens of ballplayers enshrined in the Hall of Fame filled the spots on the walls not covered with pennants. The logo of the Kansas City Monarchs could be seen on the top of the bridge table.

Throughout the poker game, Dempsey listened to Moe Franklin and the old timers debate the recent rule changes in Major League Baseball. Moe said, "Baseball just ain't like it used to be. All the things that made the game great are slowly slipping away." Henry, who looked like an older version of Morgan Freeman, chimed in, "You're right. I mean, now the league commissioner is talking about expanding the playoffs format permanently. And don't get me started about the three-batter minimum rule for pitchers, seven inning double headers, and runners starting on second base during extra innings. Baseball was such a great game the way it used to be." Bobby, who resembled comedian and game show host Steve Harvey, asked, "Why are they always attempting to fix something that was fine the way it was?" At that point, Dempsey jumped into the conversation and said, "All of these rule changes won't solve any of the real issues that Major League Baseball needs to address. If the MLB commissioner understood media, maybe the league would have a fighting chance to make things right. But right now, fans can't even watch their local teams sometimes because of the MLB rules that enforce television blackouts. Fans buy the MLB cable package to watch their favorite team and they can't even watch them play half the time. It's madness. How is the league going to increase viewership if fans can't even see the games they want to watch?"

Frank, who reminded Dempsey of actor James Earl Jones, agreed. He said, "He's right. I guess Major League Baseball makes lots of money from this business model, but they risk dissing a generation of fans." Then Henry said, "You want to keep the game of baseball popular? Don't change it. Putting a runner on second base in extra innings is not the answer. If they want to grow the game, market the players. You have more players in baseball than any other professional sport and they have more diverse backgrounds. That's the way to do it." Dempsey added, "If the owners really want to make Major League Baseball better, they should create a promotion and relegation system just like the one that exists in Europe with soccer. They should also end the MLB antitrust exemption and set MLB minor league affiliate teams free." Dempsey, who probably would have enjoyed keeping the conversation going, smiled and said, "I'm sorry, guys. I've got to get back to campus. I just got a great idea for my first lecture of the new semester, and possibly for my PhD thesis in economics as well!"

CHAPTER THREE

The Political Economy

THE FIRST SEMESTER STUDENTS WERE ALREADY in their seats when Professor Dempsey entered the lecture hall. He was wearing a colorful Nolan Ryan Houston Astros baseball jersey that he purchased in 1994, one year after the hard-throwing righthander retired from baseball. Dempsey considered Ryan one of the best pitchers of all time, and he had the credentials to support Dempsey's opinion. He still holds several Major League Baseball records, including the most career strikeouts by a pitcher (5,714), the most no-hitters (7), and the lowest batting average allowed (.204). Dempsey had another reason for wearing Ryan's jersey, which he would discuss later during his lecture on economics.

He said to the class, "Good morning, everyone, welcome to Political Economy class. I am Professor Dempsey and I am fired up to have you here. Let's get started." Following the lead of The Barber Shop, Dempsey had taken the liberty of decorating this classroom with a great deal baseball memorabilia. One side wall of the lecture hall was covered with colorful baseball pennants of former Major League Baseball teams, including the Brooklyn Dodgers, the New York Giants, the Seattle Pilots, and the Milwaukee Braves. His baseball decorations also included a painting of Larry Doby of the Cleveland Indians sliding into third base. Next to that painting was a framed team poster of the 1994 Montreal Expos. Hanging next to the Montreal Expos was a Kansas City Athletics baseball jersey, also in a frame. Clearly, Dempsey loved baseball and his extensive collection of memorabilia confirmed it.

Dempsey canvassed the lecture hall and saw every seat occupied. He noticed a female student in the third row wearing a blue and white George Brett Kansas City Royals jersey. Dempsey thought she looked like a young Natalie Portman, nodded in her direction to acknowledge her, and said, "Hey, third row, nice jersey. Glad to have another true baseball fan in the room. I think you're really going to enjoy this class."

Then Dempsey got down to business. He began his first lecture of the semester with a very technical introduction. He said, "The blend of political science and economics provides the foundation for this class. Political economists study government or organizational policies to determine how they impact the economy. Researchers study economic theories, such as capitalism, socialism, and communism, and evaluate their impact in the real world. Our field of economics draws upon sociology and political science to define the manner in which government and economic systems influence each other. Political economists examine the potential benefits and risks associated with the implementation of these policies and theories. They also examine how individuals might participate in changes. By studying the interplay between capital and labor, for example, political economists can generate policy outcomes beneficial to society. Similarly, when creating new institutions and organizations, political economists can infuse ideology into the process, which allows individuals and members of those organizations to decide what they should do to remain consistent with their basic values and beliefs. This, in a nutshell, is what political economics is all about. In this class, we are going to explore some of the notable moments at which politics and economics have intersected with professional baseball in meaningful ways. Here, you will see how politics and economics constantly crosses over into baseball, for example, in the structure of the league, in labor negotiations, in team relocations from one city to another, and in payroll policies. And I have no doubt that this intersection will continue to occur in the decades to come." Dempsey explained to his students that he planned to make learning about the political economy easier, more interesting, and hopefully more enjoyable, by using the business of baseball as a platform to teach his political and economic concepts throughout the semester.

Following his lesson plan for this lecture, Dempsey changed direction and asked if anyone in the class had any idea why he was wearing a Houston Astros jersey from the 1970s. Finding no volunteers, he explained its significance.

He told the students that while baseball in the 1970s may be most remembered as the decade of synthetic Astroturf playing surfaces, symmetrical multi-purpose stadiums with corporate suites, and carefully cultivated mustaches worn by Rollie Fingers and Goose Gossage, it was also the decade of radically designed and fashionable baseball uniforms. The Houston Astros jersey he was wearing was a perfect example. It was a colorful pullover jersey, without buttons, that the team wore for both home and away games. It featured solid blocks of horizontal red, orange, and yellow stripes from the chest down. Dempsey said, "This unique jersey design even earned itself a nickname, 'The Tequila Sunrise,' because it resembles the cocktail drink. I've always loved this jersey because it introduced the economics of fashion and design into baseball attire. But at the same time, the jersey saddens me because, in my opinion, that period of time marked the end of the first golden age of baseball."

Dempsey then changed the direction of his lecture again. He proceeded to give the class a history lesson on baseball. He explained that in 1858, sixteen ballclubs from the New York City area formed the sport's first governing body, the National Association of Baseball Players. Eventually, the game became so popular that people wanted to watch the action live in person. It didn't take long after that for local news publications to begin covering baseball games. This created good press, turned some journalists into sportswriters, and helped sell more newspapers. Baseball's popularity continued to flourish and by the 1890s, there was enough demand for "in progress" games to be broadcast by telegraph. The first sale of broadcast rights of baseball games occurred in 1897, and years later in 1913, Western Union agreed to a five-year deal for the rights to broadcast the games on the radio. Baseball club owners originally resisted this arrangement, fearing it would hurt ticket sales at the gate. To the contrary, radio became a huge source of income and free advertising for the ballclubs. It actually attracted more local fans to attend home games and non-local fans to follow their favorite teams over the airwaves. The first World Series to be aired nationally occurred a decade later in 1922. By 1950, national radio broadcasts of regular season games were added to the Liberty Broadcasting System and the big bucks started to roll in.

Dempsey's lecture on baseball history continued. He focused on the plight of African-Americans. He told the class that they began playing baseball in the late 1800s on all-black teams in the military, on corporate company teams, and, for the few lucky enough to enroll, in college. Based on talent, they eventually were permitted to join professional major league teams that previously had been white players only. Moses Fleetwood Walker and Bud Fowler were among the first African-Americans to integrate and excel. However, the advancement of black baseball players was short-lived. Racism and "Jim Crow" laws caused them to be excluded from these teams by 1900s. As a result, black players again formed their own units and went "barnstorming" all around the country to play anyone who would accept their challenge.

The last topic Dempsey discussed with the class was the formation of what is known today as Major League Baseball. He mentioned the very early years during which almost every major league that formed failed. It wasn't until the National League was founded in 1876 that baseball made its mark and began to thrive. Twenty-five years later, in 1901, the National League's first successful counterpart, the American League, which evolved from the minor Western League, was established. The two competing leagues, each with eight teams, were rivals that fought to attract the best players and fans. In 1903, after months of conflict, economics took over and the leagues agreed to merge. With the combination, the organization known as Major League Baseball was formed and professional baseball began its evolution into the multi-billion-dollar industry it is today.

Then Dempsey looked at his watch and said, "That's about it for today, everyone. We covered a lot of ground with much more to come. Read your next assignment on the antitrust exemption and come prepared to answer questions and do most of the talking at our next class." As the students walked out of the lecture hell, Dempsey thought about his busy day ahead. He had two more economics classes to teach. Then he planned to drive downtown to hit some balls to the kids at the baseball academy and make a stop in the back room of The Barber Shop. That would be followed by a return trip to campus, specifically to the third floor of the university library to delve deeper into his new idea for his PhD thesis.

CHAPTER FOUR

The Antitrust Exception

TWO DAYS LATER, PROFESSOR DEMPSEY WALKED into the lecture hall for the second Political Economy class. Dempsey was ready to discuss the history of baseball's antitrust exemption. He was dressed casually as usual, wearing a Roberto Clemente Pittsburg Pirates home jersey with blue jeans and grey tennis sneakers. The jersey was a white button-down with black and bright yellow trim and "Pirates" written across the chest. He felt properly dressed for the occasion.

Dempsey was just a kid when his dad told him all about Roberto Clemente. In addition to being a truly great ball-player during his 18 years with the Pirates, Clemente was actively involved in charity work during the off-season. He often delivered food, necessities, and baseball equipment to the under-privileged and those in need. Only 38 years old, Clemente died in a plane crash while on a trip to assist earthquake victims in Nicaragua. After learning more about Clemente's talent and generosity, Dempsey purchased his jersey to honor his memory.

To begin his lecture on baseball's antitrust exemption, Dempsey opened his laptop computer and typed in a few key strokes. When he hit the return button, the screen on his laptop projected on to a much bigger screen on the wall in the front of the classroom. What his students saw was the official website of the Federal Trade Commission at ftc.gov.

Keeping his word that his students would do most of the talking for this class, Dempsey asked for a volunteer to discuss the first few antitrust laws and their purpose. Several hands went up and Dempsey called on the young lady sitting in the center of the third row. Rachel Silver, a brown-haired, brown-eyed sophomore who played second base on her high school varsity softball team, stood up to respond. Rachel said that Congress passed the first antitrust law, The Sherman Act, in 1890. It was a comprehensive charter of economic liberty aimed at preserving free and unfettered competition as the rule of trade. She continued that Congress passed two additional antitrust laws in 1914, The Federal Trade Commission Act, which created the FTC, and The Clayton Act, which prohibited anticompetitive mergers, predatory and discriminatory pricing, and other forms of unethical corporate behavior. She said that these antitrust laws prohibited unlawful mergers and business practices and used the judicial system to resolve conflicts. She noted that these three federal antitrust laws remain in effect today, with some revisions. Looking straight at the student, Dempsey said, "That was excellent. I couldn't have explained it any better myself. Nice job."

Then Dempsey asked for another volunteer to discuss the primary objectives of these antitrust laws. More hands went up and Dempsey pointed to a young man sitting one row behind and a few seats to the right of Rachel. Corey Gordon stood up. He was a sophomore like Rachel and coincidentally was her classmate at Lee's Summit High School in Missouri. Standing at over six feet tall, with blonde hair blue eyes, and distinctively high cheekbones, he was an imposing figure. Corey explained that these antitrust laws protected balanced competition for the benefit of American citizens. They were designed to create strong incentives for businesses to operate efficiently, which created better competition and kept prices down and quality up, a result which benefited all consumers. Additionally, the antitrust laws were designed to punish those in the business community who practiced unfair or unethical competitive behavior. Corey added that the United States court system had applied these antitrust laws in litigation for decades with significant influence and dramatic impact on economic markets. Dempsey said, "That was excellent too. I'm very impressed."

At this point, Dempsey delved deeper into the details of the Sherman Act and why Major League Baseball was exempt from its application. He explained that The Sherman Act outlawed every contract, combination, or conspiracy in restraint of trade, and any monopolization, attempted monopolization, or conspiracy or combination to monopolize. He noted, however, that the U.S. Supreme

Court decided that the Sherman Act did not prohibit every restraint of trade, only those that were deemed unreasonable. On the other hand, certain actions were considered so harmful to competition that they were almost always illegal. These included arrangements among competing individuals or businesses to fix prices, divide markets, or rig bids. He highlighted that Major League Baseball was the only major sport in the U.S. exempt from these antitrust laws. Then he discussed the circumstances which gave rise to it.

Dempsey told the class that Major League Baseball's antitrust exemption surfaced in 1922 as a result of the landmark Supreme Court decision in *Federal Baseball Club v. National League*. In 1913, a group of entrepreneurs set up The Federal League of Base Ball Clubs, known as the Federal League. After its first year playing as a minor league, it operated the next two years as "the third major league" competing alongside the National League and the American League, the sport's preeminent baseball institutions at that time. Federal League clubs aggressively poached National League and American League players, enticing them to jump ship with larger contracts and friendlier labor policies. In retaliation, National League and American League owners bought and then shut down every rival Federal League team, except for one, the Baltimore Terrapins. The owners of the Terrapins, the last club standing, sued, giving rise to this federal lawsuit.

Dempsey noted that at first glance, *Federal Baseball* looked like a straightforward case because the National League and the American League did not deny that their behavior was unreasonable and monopolistic. The Supreme Court, however, ruled that baseball was exempt from antitrust law because "the business of baseball is giving exhibitions," not interstate commerce. It was a puzzling decision said Dempsey, and he wondered if the judges were bribed or threatened. Yet, even after all these years, this unanimous Supreme Court decision, written by esteemed Justice Oliver Wendell Holmes, is still the law of the land. Dempsey continued that unless another case comes up before the Supreme Court, in which the judges decide to overturn the 1922 decision, only legislation from Congress can remove Major League Baseball's unique and, in Dempsey's opinion, unjustified antitrust exemption.

Dempsey supported his opinion by explaining that free competition is essential in a capitalistic economic system. Since he was a libertarian at heart, he recognized the need for and the benefits of a political system such as a constitutional republic that has legal checks and balances to protect free markets. In this context, Dempsey mentioned *Standard Oil Co. of New Jersey v. United States*, a 1911 decision in which the Supreme Court, relying on The Sherman Act, found the oil company guilty of monopolizing the industry through a series of abusive and anticompetitive actions. After this decision, the oil exploration and refining behemoth, owned by John D. Rockefeller and his business partners, was broken up into more than thirty different, much smaller, energy companies. In further support, Dempsey also mentioned *United States v. AT&T*, the antitrust case that attacked the telephone company's use of monopolistic actions to enhance its profits. After years of litigation, the case was settled in 1982 by means of a consent decree in which the telecommunications goliath was broken up into seven different, smaller regional operating phone companies.

Finally, Dempsey asked his students if they could think of any examples of how Major League Baseball in recent years has exhibited monopolistic power. Many hands quickly went up around the classroom. Then he said, "Good. Please write a short paper about this subject and submit it to me in my office before the end of next week. I look forward to seeing everyone at our next class." Dempsey was the first person to exit the lecture hall because he had another busy afternoon ahead of him.

CHAPTER FIVE

The Plight of the Minor Leagues

PROFESSOR DEMPSEY WOKE UP BRIGHT AND early, just in time to say "have a great day" and kiss Sarah goodbye on the cheek as she walked out of the kitchen into the garage. She was on her way to an important client meeting at her office. After a shower and breakfast, Dempsey prepared for the day ahead. He walked into the guest bedroom, opened the closet door, and decided which of his more than three dozen baseball jerseys he would wear to the university campus. He chose a classic, the red/navy blue on white jersey of the defunct Colorado Springs Sky Sox. Dempsey knew it was the perfect choice for his next lecture later that morning.

Dempsey drove to the campus, went to his office, and read and graded several papers his students had written on Major League Baseball's antitrust exemption and monopolistic power. Then he picked up the stack of sports business journals on his desk that he had borrowed from the university library the previous evening. He walked down the hallway and then strolled into the lecture hall. By this time, his students realized that their economics professor probably had a different baseball jersey for every class lecture.

Dempsey told his students that while he was researching material for his PhD thesis, he came across some very interesting financial data and economic analysis related to baseball. He pulled out his notes and shared the following with the class. According to *Forbes* magazine, the average valuation of every Major League Baseball team had grown by almost $140 million every single year over the last decade. Even the smallest market with the lowest valuation, the Kansas City Royals, had seen its valuation jump on average $71 million each year. During this time span, the average value of a major league franchise increased 365%, from $523 million to $1.91 billion. The average salary of major league ballplayers also increased during this period, but only by about 12%. Per *Forbes*, the average ballclub payroll in 2011 was roughly $93 million and was expected to increase to around $104 million in 2021. Dempsey was certain that the obvious disparity of the economic benefits realized by owners and players during this decade was not lost on his students.

Dempsey pointed out that some of the best baseball players did quite well. He gave a few striking examples. In 2019, Mike Trout signed a 12-year, $426 million contract with the Los Angeles Angels and Mookie Betts signed a 12-year $365 million contract with the Los Angeles Dodgers. More recently, Juan Soto signed a $440 million contract extension after being traded to the San Diego Padres. He emphasized that Betts was exceptional and Trout was considered by many to be the best ballplayer alive today. Soto, on the other hand, was only 23 years old with much yet to prove on the ballfield. Soto's contract led Dempsey to wonder how much Aaron Judge, Shohei Ohtani, and Jacob deGrom might garner when they became free agents.

Then Dempsey changed the direction of his lecture to focus on the economics of minor league baseball. He began with some success stories. First, he mentioned the Sacramento River Cats franchise, the Triple-A minor league affiliate of the San Francisco Giants valued at $49 million. The River Cats amassed some of the most consistently successful attendance and revenue numbers in minor league baseball averaging more than 9,000 fans per game. They play their home games at Raley Field, a $29.5 million ballpark built in 2000, which has generated $11.5 million in annual ticket sales representing more than 50% of the team's revenues. Then he mentioned other successful minor league franchises, including the Charlotte Knights, the Triple-A affiliate of the Chicago White Sox, the El Paso Chihuahuas, the Triple-A affiliate of the San Diego Padres, and the Dayton Dragons, an affiliate of the Cincinnati Reds. Since opening their new ballpark in 2014, the Charlotte Knights have averaged more than 9,400 fans per game, the highest in the minor leagues, and the team is estimated to be worth $47 million. The franchise has earned an annual profit of $5 million per season on approximately $17 million in revenue. It is estimated that the Chihuahuas in the Pacific Coast League are worth $38 million. The Dragons, estimated to be worth $45 million, earned more than $6 million in annual profit in 2021.

Dempsey emphasized, however, that all is not well in the minor leagues. Generally speaking, life in the minors is difficult for young ballplayers. They travel long distances by bus, not by air. They stay in motels, not 4-star hotels. They usually eat fast food, not high-quality food. On top of that, salaries are low and health benefits meager. And it went from bad to worse for minor league teams and players as a result of the Covid-19 pandemic. While the major league baseball season in 2020 was initially delayed and ultimately reduced to just 60 games from the traditional 162, games were still played, albeit without fans in the stands. Conversely, the commissioner of Major League Baseball decided unilaterally to cancel the entire minor league season. This was a devastating blow to minor league ballplayers, many of whom did not get paid, and to minor league teams, forcing many to fire staff and incur tremendous financial loses. Dempsey asked the class if that seemed fair. No student responded to his rhetorical question.

Continuing his lesson on minor league economics, Dempsey noted that, following MLB's shutdown of its season in March of 2020, more than one hundred minor league baseball teams were banished into sports purgatory. Teams that were not profitable had to settle debts and return thousands of dollars in advertising revenue to sponsors and advance ticket sales to fans. Some teams were forced to fire employees and several retained just one person to handle what was left of day-to-day team operations. Many minor league teams had to accept the federal government's small business loans through the Paycheck Protection Program known as "PPP Money."

To end the lecture, Dempsey went on to discuss what he described as the unusual financial arrangement that exists between major and minor league franchises. He explained that, due to strict and somewhat arcane rules, major league baseball teams were not allowed to financially support or pump funds into their affiliates, even as they suffered economically from their cancelled season, because they do not own them. The majority of these affiliates are owned by private citizens and businesses. As a result of this surprising ownership structure, Major League Baseball teams were in no position to help their minor league counterparts at the most critical time. Without substantial financial assistance from the private sector, a few minor league clubs had to shutter operations and file for bankruptcy protection. Dempsey called this arrangement absurd since the primary goal of the minor league system is to develop and prepare young ballplayers to play in the major leagues. After pausing a few seconds to let his last statements sink in, Dempsey said, "Well, that's it for today, everyone. Please read the assignment for next week's class and be prepared to discuss the economics of labor. Enjoy the weekend."

Dempsey went to his office, briefly reviewed his material for the next class, graded the rest of the papers his students had written on baseball's monopoly, and called Sarah to say hello and see what was on her agenda. She told him that she would be working late so he was free for the evening. Dempsey decided to find out what was going on at The Barber Shop.

Walking in the front door of the store, Dempsey saw Moe talking with a customer interested in purchasing Derek Jeter's rookie card. That would be a nice sale for Moe thought Dempsey. He nodded hello and walked into the back room and saw Henry, Frank and Bobby playing baseball card poker again. He sat in Moe's chair but didn't join the game. Instead, he asked the old timers if they had any idea how many minor league baseball teams recently went bankrupt or were on the verge of bankruptcy.

Bobby shook his head as if he knew all about it, and said, "I am well aware of the situation, but I don't know the number. What I do know from my relatives is that the Jackson Generals in Tennessee, the Staten Island Yankees, and the Charlotte Stone Crabs in Florida are all gone. It's a damn shame." Frank chimed in, "Well, I think those teams, and any others that are gone, should get together and sue Major League Baseball. Sue them for antitrust. MLB cancelled their season without them having any say on the matter. Jobs were lost, business got hurt, and local communities suffered. Just like Bobby said, it's a damn shame." Before Dempsey could put in his two cents, Henry said, "You're both right. I think that the Generals and the Stone Crabs should sue Major League Baseball and, after they win, they should start their own baseball league." Moe, who was now leaning against the frame of the doorway to the back room and overheard the conversation, said, "I agree with you, Henry. Just imagine how liberating it would be if all the minor league teams were set free from the shackles of Major League Baseball and created their own professional baseball league." Dempsey smiled and made a thankful prayer gesture as he looked up to the ceiling realizing that Henry and Frank's comment sparked another idea in his mind.

CHAPTER SIX

The Disenfranchised Baseball Player

PROFESSOR DEMPSEY WAS UP BEFORE THE ALARM AND the sunrise and was ready to leave the house when Sarah, still in her pajamas, entered the kitchen. Dempsey was anxious to get to the university library long before his first class to research his new idea for his PhD thesis. A little over an hour later, that's just where he was and where he spent the next few hours. Taking a break from reading, he looked at his Apple iPhone and realized it was time to go. He knew he had to get to his office, pick up his slide projector, and set it up in the lecture hall before his students arrived.

Usually his students were already in their seats when Dempsey entered the lecture hall, but not this day. Today, he was leaning against the front wall waiting for them to stroll in. He was wearing an orange and black jersey of the Salem-Keizer Volcanoes, another victim of the Covid-19 pandemic and the canceled 2020 minor league season. Once again, Dempsey knew it was the appropriate attire for the day's subject matter.

After the students were in their seats, Dempsey said, "Today we are going to talk about the economics of labor. While the game of baseball employs many different kinds of workers, from security guards to beer salesmen, from field maintenance personnel to scouts, today's discussion will focus on the workers at the center of the profession, the baseball players, specifically those laboring in the minor leagues." Dempsey asked, "Did you know that unlike major league ballplayers, minor leaguers are not allowed to form a union?" Rachel Silver, raised her hand to speak and responded to Dempsey's question with a question of her own. "Why would MLB's players union not include minor leaguers as well, or at least support the formation of a union of their own?" Then Corey Gordon raised his hand to speak and Dempsey's nod in his direction gave him the floor. Corey said that he had no problem with traditional unions that truly benefit their members. However, for several reasons, he had a problem with many unions in America today and gave examples. Some modern unions at big companies force workers to join and pay dues as a condition of employment. Others use tactics to block rival unions from forming. And some, typically run by professional teamsters, often use union dues to support a political agenda. As for major league ballplayers, he said that they actually have a pretty good union. However, it was ridiculous that minor leaguers cannot be part of the same union, especially since that's where all major leaguers come from when they get called up to "the show." He concluded that if minor leaguers cannot become members of the MLB Players Association, they certainly should be allowed to form their own union.

After Corey completed his rant, Dempsey asked the class if anyone else had an opinion on this complex labor issue. RJ Shah, a handsome young man with straight black hair, brown eyes, and a trimmed beard sitting in the center of the last row of the lecture hall, raised his hand to comment. RJ, an international student from Mumbai, India, in his second year at UMKC, whose father was a professional cricket coach, said, "It is ironic to me that baseball is 'America's pastime.' Major League Baseball is not even capitalistic. The league is one big privately-owned company. It's a monopoly protected by Congress and the Supreme Court and its internal economic system is not based on free market capitalism as Adam Smith described in his book, *The Wealth of Nations*. I would argue that Major League Baseball is run more like an authoritarian dictatorship politically and economically, its system closely resembles communism. Under a communist system, such as those in Cuba and China, the citizens suffer. Major League Baseball is a centrally planned economy run by the commissioner's office. It is really a monopoly wrapped around an oligopoly of just thirty franchise owners. Even their amateur draft system, the Rule 5 draft, and their fixed salaries for minor league players are forms of socialism or communism."

Dempsey smiled indicating that he clearly enjoyed, and no doubt agreed, with Shah's diatribe. He said, "Bravo to you, Mr. Shah. And well done to you as well, Ms. Silver and

Mr. Gordon. You all made good points. Now let's take a closer look at just how poorly Major League Baseball treats minor league players." Dempsey walked a few steps to the projector he had set up before class and clicked the first slide of his presentation. It referenced a July 8, 2019 article written by sports journalist Daniel Gallen from *Patriot News* entitled "Minor league baseball salaries hover at poverty level while major league teams earn big profits." The article was part of the reading material Dempsey had assigned for this lecture so he was sure that his students were familiar with its content. Nevertheless, he wanted to highlight the severe economic burden minors league ballplayers endure.

Referencing Gallen's article, he noted that as of 2018, the average salary for a minor league baseball player during the regular season, which is contractually pre-arranged by Major League Baseball, starts at around $6,000 per season in Single-A, grows to about $9,350 per season in Double-A, and increases to nearly $15,000 a year in Triple-A. Surprisingly, minor leaguers do not even get paid during spring training. Finally, the article pointed out that the vast majority of minor league baseball players earn an annual wage below the poverty line, which according to the U.S. Department of Health and Human Services was $12,490 in 2019. This situation still exists today. As a result, said Dempsey, many minor league ballplayers take on second and third jobs during the offseason to makes ends meet.

Dempsey clicked to the next slide in his presentation and said, "You're going to get a kick out of this one, especially the title." It read "Save America's Pastime Act," an ironically Orwellian name chosen by congressional lawmakers.

He told the class that the piece of legislation was included in the 2018 economic spending bill passed by Congress. Shockingly, it modified the Fair Labor Standards Act of 1938 to strip minor leaguers of minimum wage protection. He said, "Since baseball's antitrust exemption has been in place since 1922 and because minor league baseball players don't have union protection, they were helpless to fight the new law. You can't make this stuff up. Furthermore, management's tight grip on the baseball labor force is not limited to the minor leaguers, although that's where the economics are most extreme."

Dempsey explained that even though major league ballplayers do have a union, they are still oppressed by Major League Baseball team owners. For example, after a team drafts a player into the league, the franchise that selected him owns "the rights" to that player. Since the thirty MLB teams work together as a cartel, that ballplayer has no other alternative but to negotiate and sign a contract with the franchise that drafted him. Further shackling that ballplayer, the team owns his rights for six years before that player can elect free agency and sign with a different ballclub. Up until St. Louis Cardinal outfielder Curt Flood got the ball rolling with litigation in 1970 attacking the reserve clause in MLB contracts, players had no bargaining power with the team owners at all. Players were bound to one team forever, subject to the whims of the owner in negotiating their salary and possibly being traded to another team in another city. Fortunately, the reserve clause in contracts was abolished in 1975, replaced by free agency. Baseball players have been thanking Curt Flood ever since.

Dempsey showed the class several more interesting slides on the economics of labor before declaring time up, lecture over. He pointed directly at Rachel, Corey, and RJ and said, "You three, great work once again. For our next class, I'm throwing you all a curve ball. Be prepared to learn about the economics of liberty."

As the students filed out of the lecture hall, Dempsey mentioned that the youth baseball team that he coached had a game that evening at 6 p.m. at the Kansas City Urban Youth Baseball Academy and invited his students to attend and watch some quality baseball. He also invited the class to The Barber Shop on Friday night for a baseball card poker tournament Moe Franklin was hosting. He didn't think he would have any takers but was inclined to wait and see.

CHAPTER SEVEN

The Economics of Liberty

PROFESSOR DEMPSEY ARRIVED EARLY ON CAMPUS again. He was wearing his white Hank Greenberg Detroit Tigers baseball jersey, another one of his favorite outfits. He set up the projector in the lecture hall, grabbed a piece of chalk off of his desk, and wrote the word "Liberty" in large capital letters on the chalkboard. He said, "I suspect that many of you might think that the foundation of a successful economic model begins with natural resources such as timber, coal and oil. However, I suggest to you that the foundation actually begins with liberty. I'm sure you all read the material assigned in preparation for this class and I hope that you'll appreciate the significance of economic liberty by the time you leave the lecture hall today."

Dempsey walked over to the projector and clicked on the first slide. It was a picture of a portrait of a man with long, grey hair that he was certain his students did not recognize.

It was John Locke, an English physician and philosopher who lived in the 17th century. He was considered one of most influential and enlightened thinkers of his time. Dempsey explained that Locke believed that all individuals were equal in the sense that they were born with certain inalienable natural rights, meaning rights that were God-given and could not be taken or even given away. According to Locke, these fundamental rights were life, liberty, and property. Locke believed that individuals should be free to make choices about how to conduct their own lives as long as they did not interfere with the liberty of others. By "property," Locke meant more than land and goods that could be purchased, sold, or given away. He also believed that property referred to ownership of oneself, which included the right to personal well-being, the right to pursue work, and the right to be paid fair wages for that work.

Dempsey clicked to the next slide which showed side-by-side portraits of Patrick Henry, a familiar face in American history and a Founding Father of the United States, and of Lemuel Haynes, a face less familiar to his students. Both were patriots who fought during the American Revolution to secure independence from British rule. Henry, an attorney and politician, is best known for his famous declaration at the Second Virginia Convention in 1775, "Give me liberty, or give me death," a statement he often repeated in his political speeches and writings after independence was achieved. The lesser-known patriot Hayes, was a clergyman who became the first black man in the United States to be ordained as a minister. Dempsey then read aloud the following, quoting Hayes, "Liberty and freedom is an innate principle, which is unmovably placed in the human species; and to see a man aspire after it, is not enigmatical, seeing he acts no ways incompatible with his own nature. Liberty is a jewel which was handed down to man from the cabinet of heaven."

The last slide showed by Dempsey was a portrait of Thomas Jefferson, another Founding Father and the 3rd president of the United States elected in 1801. Everyone in the class recognized him immediately. Twenty-five years before Jefferson began his service as president, he was the principal author of the Declaration of Independence. As he did with Hayes, Dempsey quoted aloud Jefferson's language from the second paragraph of that famous document, "We hold these truths to be self-evident, that all men are created equal, that they are endowed by their Creator with certain unalienable rights, that among these are Life, Liberty and the pursuit of Happiness." Dempsey explained that most scholars and historians who study the Declaration of Independence believe that Jefferson derived his most well-known ideas from the writings of John Locke. Dempsey also said that Locke wrote about liberty, freedom, and equality in his Second Treatise of Government in 1689 at the time of England's "Glorious Revolution" to overthrow the rule of King James II. That was almost a century before Jefferson penned the Declaration of Independence.

Dempsey shut off the slide projector and asked the class for their thoughts on the presentation. Several students offered their opinions. After the open discussion, and to conclude the class, Dempsey gave his students their second written assignment of the semester. He granted the class one week to write an essay on "The Economics of Liberty, John Locke, and Major League Baseball."

Strolling out of the lecture hall, RJ turned to Rachel and Corey and said, "Hey guys, when you signed up for this Political Economy course, did you know how much of the material would be about baseball?" Corey replied, "No, but I love that it is. Professor Dempsey makes learning about politics and economics fun." Rachel agreed, smiled, and said, "Best class ever."

CHAPTER EIGHT

The Invisible Hand

FOR HIS NEXT POLITICAL ECONOMY CLASS, PROFESSOR Dempsey walked into the classroom wearing a grey Lou Gehrig New York Yankees jersey with his number 4 on the back. Gehrig played 17 seasons for the Yankees, almost always batting fourth in the lineup behind the legendary Babe Ruth. He was renowned for his clutch hitting and for his durability, which earned him the nickname "The Iron Horse." His record of playing 2,130 consecutive games was considered unbreakable until it was surpassed 56 years later by the great Baltimore Orioles shortstop Cal Ripken, Jr. Dempsey recalled having paid a little extra for Gehrig's jersey at a baseball memorabilia trade show, but as a true baseball fan, he felt that it was money well spent. Plus, he remembered the high praise Gehrig received from his grandfather on the Dempsey family farm in Wichita.

Dempsey greeted his students with a smile and did a little

spin to show off his Gehrig jersey. He said, "Even though my grandfather lived in Kansas, Lou Gehrig was his favorite baseball player. He told me that Babe Ruth got most of the attention because of all of the home runs he hit, but gramps always wondered how many fewer dingers Ruth would have hit if he didn't have The Iron Horse in the on-deck circle hitting behind him. I didn't realize it at the time, but that conversation was my first lesson about statistics. They don't always tell the whole story."

After that introduction, Dempsey began his presentation and prepared remarks for the day. He turned and wrote the words "The Invisible Hand" in very large letters on the blackboard, so large that the students sitting in the last row of the lecture hall had no trouble reading them. Then he underlined the phrase three times for emphasis. Dempsey turned around, faced his students, and told them that today's class would focus on free-market capitalism. The professor lectured saying that "The Invisible Hand" was an economic metaphor first introduced in the 18th-century by Adam Smith. Smith was a Scottish philosopher and economist known by many as "The Father of Capitalism" and by others as "The Father of Economics." Smith wrote *The Wealth of Nations* in 1776, which is considered the first modern dissertation on the subject of economics.

Dempsey continued noting that according to Smith, "The Invisible Hand" was the mechanism through which beneficial social and economic outcomes arose due to the accumulated self-interested actions of individuals, none of whom intended to bring about those outcomes. The concept needed a free market to work properly since it relied on the voluntary exchange of goods and services. The voluntary nature of the transaction ensured that both parties benefitted, as either participant could refuse the exchange and accept only an offer that suited his or her interests. Dempsey said that Smith believed that a truly free market could only exist without the interference of government control, as it must behave spontaneously in order to thrive. A free market economy, fueled by the laws of supply and demand and voluntary business decisions, motivated businesses to provide goods and services that met public needs in return for a profit. Dempsey concluded the discussion saying, "That's a lot to digest, I know, but the concept demonstrates that Adam Smith knew what he was writing about and that his nickname as the 'Father of Capitalism' was well earned."

Dempsey turned to the blackboard again and did his very best to draw the yin and yang symbols, signs that are more well known in Asian cultures. The symbols showed a balance between two opposites, with a portion of the opposite element in each section. Dempsey turned, faced the class, and continued his lecture saying that the free market allows two individuals to both reap mutually beneficial gains from trade, essentially balancing out each other just like the yin and the yang. Dempsey went on to question whether government interventions, such as subsidies, bailouts, licensing, taxes, and other selective corporate privileges, distort the flow of information and incentives that lead entrepreneurs to find opportunities to create mutual benefit for themselves and others. He also worried that when corporations collude with governments, free markets get corrupted, which he believed would lead to controlled pricing, hindered competition, and prevent public needs from being met.

Circling back to a previous lecture, Dempsey discussed the relationship between Adam Smith's "Free Markets" concept and John Locke's "Economics of Liberty" theory. He said, "Regulations often shield incumbent businesses from competition. Since government interventions benefit some at the expense of others, they create incentives for unprincipled alliances. This typically leads to what is called 'crony capitalism,' which is anything but real capitalism. I think crony capitalism is fascism or communism in disguise and these nefarious political influences damage the free markets that Smith envisioned. Why you might ask? Because political ideologies, such as fascism, Marxism, or communism, definitely infringe, in one way or another, on an individual's personal liberty." To conclude, Dempsey gave his students their next assignment. He asked them to write a short, two-page essay on the application of Adam Smith's Free Markets theory to Major League Baseball.

At that point, RJ looked at Rachel and Corey who were packing up their belongings. He said to them jokingly, "This class just keeps getting better and better. By the time this semester is over, I suspect Professor Dempsey will have us thinking that baseball is the most important economic indicator, more important than inflation, unemployment, trade and GDP."

CHAPTER NINE

The Theory of Creative Destruction

PROFESSOR DEMPSEY AWOKE BEFORE THE ALARM to the sound of very heavy rain beating against his bedroom window. He got up looking for Sarah but she was already gone. Her note on the kitchen table read, "Left really early this morning. Important meeting this afternoon to prepare for. It's pouring cats and dogs. Be sure to take your raincoat to campus today. See you tonight. Love you." Despite the weather report, Dempsey was in his car about an hour later on his way downtown to The Barber Shop. He and Moe Franklin had some serious baseball card memorabilia to discuss.

It was still pouring when Dempsey and Moe completed their business. His ride from the baseball card store to the university campus took much longer than usual. Typically, about 15 minutes, the drive took over an hour. He had to contend with heavy traffic, some local street flooding, and a bad 3-car accident on Broadway near Country Club Plaza. The accident required him, and every other driver, to detour on to less traveled local streets. As a result, for the first time in his teaching career, Dempsey was late for class.

Waiting in the lecture hall for their professor's arrival, Rachel turned to Corey sitting in the row behind her and said, "Ok, I'll bet you twenty bucks that Professor Dempsey is wearing another baseball jersey today and it will be a jersey of someone who played in the National League." Corey replied, "You're on, I'll take that bet. I think he'll be wearing another American League jersey today." RJ overheard their conversation and chimed in, "He wore Lou Gehrig's American League jersey to our last class." Wanting to join in on the wagering, RJ said, "Anyone want to bet that not only will Professor Dempsey be wearing an American League jersey, but I think he will repeat that Lou Gehrig jersey because of his affection for his grandfather." Rachel finished the conversation saying, "No way this baseball fanatic repeats that jersey today, or any jersey this entire semester. For twenty bucks, you're on RJ. I'll take that bet." Rachel, Corey, and RJ all did a thumb's up motion just as Dempsey opened the door and entered the lecture hall.

The buzz of class chatter quieted down. Dempsey walked in completely drenched, with his rain coat dripping a trail of water on the floor as he walked across the room toward the closet. He said, "Everyone, please forgive me for being late to class. I was downtown at The Barber Shop negotiating a trade with Moe Franklin for a classic 1964 Willie Mays baseball card I want to give to my dad for his birthday. Mays was his favorite ballplayer and I'm sure he will be thrilled to receive it." Realizing that Dempsey had just revealed another layer of his personality to his students, Rachel, Corey, and RJ looked at each other, smiled, and awaited Dempsey's next move.

They were not disappointed. Dempsey did his best impression of Fred Rogers, who was the host of the educational children's television show *Mister Rogers' Neighborhood* for more than three decades. He slowly took off his wet raincoat, shook it to remove excess water, and carefully hung it in the closet. Doing so revealed that he was wearing a Lenny Dykstra, home white, blue pinstripe, New York Mets jersey, with his number 4 on the back. Rachel turned around and silently cheered with a fist pump to celebrate her winning bets. She sheepishly smiled when she saw the looks on Corey and RJ's faces for betting wrong.

Dempsey began his lecture for the day by asking the class if anyone had ever heard the phrase "Creative Destruction" before reading their assignment for today. He was pretty confident that none had. This was confirmed when nobody raised a hand. Then he asked if anyone ever heard the name Joseph Schumpeter before. Again, not one person raised their hand. "Well then," he said jokingly, "Today is your lucky day."

He told his students that Schumpeter, an Austrian political economist, was the Finance Minister of German-Austria in 1919. In 1932 he emigrated to the United States to teach economics at Harvard University. Seven years later, he became a U.S. citizen. Three years after that, during his tenure at Harvard, he coined the term creative destruction. According to Schumpeter, creative destruction described an organic and dynamic process that occurred in free markets as a result of capitalistic development and business cycles. In an ever-flowing, ever-changing organic ecosystem of voluntary exchanges of goods and services that the professor envisioned, many fluctuating dynamics were constantly reshaped or replaced by entrepreneurship, innovation and competition. As implied by the word destruction, the process inevitably resulted in winners and losers. Schumpeter theorized that companies committed to older technologies experienced a decline in market share and profits. Meanwhile, free-thinking entrepreneurs created new companies and trained their employees to work with new technologies. These companies succeeded and inevitably gained market share. Companies that did not adapt to the changing times, or didn't change quickly enough, eventually lost value and possibly went out of business.

Dempsey gave a simple example of creative destruction in the U.S. economy. He said that when Henry Ford introduced assembly line innovation in 1913, this new manufacturing technology revolutionized the automobile industry and changed the transportation industry forever. While Ford's invention dramatically increased the standard of living for society at large, it also displaced, then replaced, an older business, horse buggy manufacturing and distribution. Dempsey indicated that over the last three decades, the internet had become the dominant economic force of creative destruction. Companies such as Apple, Microsoft, Google, Amazon, Netflix, Expedia, and Uber had dramatically changed the landscape of their industries and the global economy. He said that these companies will continue to do so, that is, until creative destruction finds them.

The main theme of Dempsey's lecture was that creative destruction is a natural part of the life cycle of a vibrant, healthy, free-flowing economic system. Some corporations adapt to changing market environments and some do not. The market capitalizations of companies that do will rise while those that don't will fall. Some companies will go bankrupt and disappear. He explained that the end result, while chaotic at times, is a never-ending upward trend of economic growth and higher standards of living through innovation and improved technology. As a final thought on the subject of creative destruction, Dempsey suggested that his students research the ten largest companies in the U.S. by market value in 1970 and do the same for 2021. Dempsey knew that not one of the companies on the 1970 list would be on the 2021 list.

Before dismissing the class, Dempsey reminded his students that he expected their completed assignments on Adam Smith's free market theory and John Locke's economics of liberty concept on his desk by the end of the next class. As the students walked out of the lecture hall, Corey turned to Rachel and said, "Ok, double or nothing Dempsey wears an American League jersey next class." Rachel looked at him with confidence and said, "You're on. Now I'm heading off to the library to complete that assignment." RJ and Corey agreed to join Rachel and followed her out of the lecture hall.

Dempsey removed his surprisingly still damp raincoat out of the lecture hall closet and headed for the university parking lot. He called Sarah from the car to make plans for the evening. Her secretary said she was still in a meeting and expected her to be there for some time. When Dempsey got home, he knew there would be plenty of time before Sarah walked through the door. He strolled into the kitchen, sat down at the table in front of his laptop computer, put on his headphones, played John Fogerty's song *Centerfield* on repeat, and did some additional research on his PhD thesis.

CHAPTER TEN

The Perils of Central Planning

AFTER BREAKFAST THE NEXT DAY, SARAH WAS again quickly out the door on her way to the office. Professor Dempsey took a little longer in the house before leaving. Based on the subject matter of his lecture for the day, he knew exactly what to wear. A little more than an hour later, the professor walked into the lecture hall sporting a replica of the red jersey of the national baseball team of Cuba. He turned, stepped up to the blackboard, wrote "Communism" in big uppercase letters, turned back around, and told the class that his discussion today would not involve baseball. Instead, the lecture would focus exclusively on the communistic economic model of "central planning," its perils, and a comparison of this approach to other economics theories discussed in his previous lectures.

Dempsey told the class that according to the financial website Investopedia.com, a centrally planned economy, also known as a "command economy," is an economic system in which a central authority, such as a government, makes the economic decisions regarding the manufacturing and distribution of products. Centrally planned economies were different from capitalistic market economies, where such decisions are traditionally made by businesses and consumers, because they generally ignored the realities of supply and demand dynamics in the marketplace.

Then Dempsey discussed Ludwig von Mises, one of the most influential Austrian economists of his era. Von Mises, who wrote and lectured extensively on the impact of economics on society, was best known for his work comparing communism and capitalism. He argued that command economies were untenable and doomed to fail because no rational pricing mechanism could emerge without competition and private ownership of the means of production. His theory was supported by the fact that centrally planned economic decisions made by communist governments throughout history, at least up to that period in time, were proof that authoritarian economic policies led to massive shortages and unnecessary surpluses throughout the economy.

Von Mises was an advocate of "laissez-faire" economics and a staunch opponent of all forms of communism, socialism, fascism, or any type of government system based on authoritarianism. Known for his devotion to the principles of free markets and opposition to government economic intervention, von Mises contended that a free-market economy, where the choices of consumers and entrepreneurs operated through the laws of supply and demand for consumer goods, capital goods, and labor, was the most effective system to manufacture, price, and distribute the economic goods and services desired by consumers. He believed that government intervention in the economy produced unintended consequences that often harmed the very people the government claimed it intended to help.

Dempsey then referenced Milton Friedman, the brilliant economist and statistician who received the Nobel Memorial Prize in Economic Science in 1976. Like von Mises, Friedman also believed that the perils of communism and central planning were real. He believed that for command economies to operate, rational decision making by buyers and sellers must be suppressed and therefore infringed upon an individual's liberty. Dempsey's reference to Friedman and liberty led to a class discussion of the differences between a centrally planned economy and other economic systems.

As his students got up from their seats, Dempsey said, "Please be sure to hand in your assignment due today. You can give it to me now, as you leave, or you can bring it to my office before the end of the day." Rachel, Corey and RJ, who had completed the assignment the day before, collected their belongings, handed their papers to Professor Dempsey, and headed out of the lecture hall and into the hallway. Because Dempsey did not wear an American League jersey to class, he wore the Cuba national team baseball jersey, Corey lost his double-or-nothing bet with Rachel. He turned to Rachel in defeat and said, "I'll Venmo you the cash, unless you prefer crypto." Rachel responded, "I'll take cash, thank you."

CHAPTER ELEVEN

The Empowerment of Direct Democracy

IT WAS ONE OF THOSE RARE DAYS WHEN Professor Dempsey left for work before Sarah. He arrived on campus very early and may have been the first person in the building. He went to his office and spent a couple of hours grading the assignments his students recently handed in. He was impressed. These were bright kids who appeared to grasp economic concepts quickly. Then he headed to the library to continue research on his PhD thesis. He felt like he was making progress and wanted the good vibes and momentum to continue. About two hours later, he was off to his Political Economy class.

On his way to the lecture hall, Dempsey wondered if his students would appreciate the significance of the baseball jersey he chose to wear this morning. It was a white Jackie Robinson Brooklyn Dodgers jersey with his now famous number 42 on the back. Robinson broke the color barrier in 1947 when he became the first African American in the modern era to play baseball in the major leagues. If it were not for Jackie Robinson, baseball legends like Hank Aaron, Frank Robinson and Willie Mays may never have made it to the big leagues.

Dempsey entered the lecture hall and was surprised to see that he was not the only person wearing a baseball jersey. To his complete astonishment, every student in the class was wearing one. Rachel wore a white Kansas City Royals Brett Phillips jersey with blue trim, Corey wore a black and yellow Wichita State jersey, and RJ wore a white pinstriped Iowa Cubs jersey. Unbeknownst to Dempsey, Rachel had organized a pilgrimage to The Barber Shop over the weekend and every student in the class purchased a baseball jersey. Moe Franklin had to be pleased with his good fortune and would, no doubt, thank Dempsey the next time he was in the store. Dempsey, thrilled with their cleverness, smiled and told his students that he loved their outfits.

Then Dempsey opened his laptop to the topic of the day, "Direct Democracy." He told the class that a direct democracy political system is a purer form of democracy in which the electorate decides on policy initiatives without legislative representatives as proxies. This differed from the majority of currently established democracies, which were representative democracies where people voted for representatives who then enacted policy initiatives on behalf of its citizens.

Dempsey noted that in a direct democracy, the people decide on policies without any intermediary. Depending on the particular system, this might entail passing executive decisions, making laws, and even directly electing or dismissing officials. He said that such an arrangement was still a democracy, with regional representatives just like our current system, but the political format gave even more power to the people to establish policy and make decisions that affected the economy.

Dempsey continued his lecture saying that Switzerland was a good example of a modern-era direct democracy with citizen-lawmaking. During the past 120 years, more than two hundred initiatives have been put to referendums there. The populace had proven to be conservative, approving only about 10% of these initiatives. Another modern-day direct democracy exists within the Crow Nation, a Native American tribe located in Montana. The tribe established a general council formed of all voting-age members with the authority to create legally-binding decisions through referendums.

Corey raised his hand to make a comment and Dempsey gave him the floor. Corey said, “Direct democracy gives more power to the people. It’s got a real libertarian feel to it. I love it. Imagine a world where everyone could vote directly from their mobile devices using blockchain technology. The voting system could be safe, secure, and, most importantly, transparent.” Rachel raised her hand and added, “Imagine a world where citizens could remove governors, mayors, or judges with a vote from their iPhones or laptops.” RJ chimed in, “I can imagine a world where citizens could propose the removal of unjust laws easily and quickly.” Following up on these thoughtful comments, Dempsey pondered aloud, "Can you imagine a professional baseball league that was governed by a direct democracy system? Fans would have the power that is now held by owners and the league commissioner. For example, the fans could vote to reject new rule changes that adversely affected the integrity of the game. They could even vote on the length of player suspensions after a bench clearing brawl or for the use of performance enhancing drugs."

To conclude the class, Dempsey told his students that he had completed his review of their written assignments and their grades were available on his university website. Then he gave them another assignment, a thought piece describing how they would manage a baseball league using direct democracy concepts. Finally, he thanked them for their baseball jersey surprise.

Rachel, Corey and RJ walked out of the lecture hall together. Rachel said to them, "Professor Dempsey wore a Jackie Robinson jersey today. So cool." Corey replied, "He's got to be the best professor ever."

CHAPTER TWELVE

The Philosophy of Conscious Capitalism

SEVERAL YEARS AGO, THE DEMPSEY'S FLEW TO New Orleans for business and a vacation. Sarah, there on business, attended a two-day American Bar Association conference to satisfy her annual legal education requirement. This was needed to maintain her Kansas and Missouri law licenses. Professor Dempsey, there for pleasure, went to Metairie, a suburb west of New Orleans, to catch a baseball game. He went to the Shrine on Airline, the home field of the New Orleans Baby Cakes, a minor league Triple-A affiliate of the Miami Marlins. On the second day of Sarah's ABA conference, Dempsey went back to the Shrine to watch another ballgame. During that game, he purchased a New Orleans Baby Cakes jersey at the team store. It was white, trimmed appropriately in bright Mardi Gras colors of purple, green, and gold. The Dempseys spent the next two days taking in the sights, the sounds, and the wonderful restaurants in the "Big Easy" before heading home.

Dempsey wore that New Orleans Baby Cakes baseball jersey when he entered the lecture hall for his next class lecture. Before delving into the concept of "Conscious Capitalism," the subject matter for the day, Dempsey shared his New Orleans vacation experience with his students and told them how he came to own the jersey. He said that his purchase must have been preordained because, a few years later, the New Orleans Baby Cakes relocated to Wichita, the place where he grew up and learned to play baseball. The team is now known as the Wichita Wind Surge, a Double-A affiliate of the Minnesota Twins.

Then, with the projector and screen in place, Dempsey opened his laptop, pressed a key, and presented the first slide of his lecture. It showed the logo of Whole Foods Markets, the popular multinational supermarket chain known for its sale of organic, preservative-free food selections. He referenced John Mackey, co-founder of the company, and Professor Raj Sisodia, a founding member of the conscious capitalism movement. Mackey and Sisodia co-authored a book on the subject and defined it as a way of thinking about capitalism and business that better reflected where they believe society was in the human journey and the state of our world today. According to the authors, the concept was not dissimilar to the traditional economic model known as capitalism in the sense that there was still a pursuit of profit. However, the model emphasized doing so in a way that seriously considered the interests of all principal stakeholders. The philosophy of conscious capitalism recognized that some stakeholders, such as the environment, cannot speak for themselves but still must be considered when business decisions were made. While profits are essential for a vital and sustainable business, companies that embraced a conscious capitalism model sought a higher purpose in their pursuits of profits. These companies concentrated on optimizing value for all of their stakeholders, not only their owners. This included customers, employees, suppliers, the local community, the environment, as well as shareholders. Dempsey said that institutions and organizations that embraced the concept, including baseball and other sports leagues, created value for all stakeholders and inspired actions that contributed to a conscious culture of trust, care, and cooperation.

Dempsey continued explaining that many publicly traded companies in recent years have embraced conscious capitalism. He clicked the keys on his computer three more times and the logos of Starbucks, The Container Store, and Southwest Airlines appeared in succession. He said that these companies, and many others, enjoyed the benefits of this philosophical approach to doing business. He spent the next few minutes discussing the business models of each company.

Dempsey finished his lecture noting that the benefits that accrued to businesses that practiced conscious capitalism include an increase in harmony between employers and employees, a higher level of employee and customer satisfaction, enhanced stakeholder loyalty, heightened community engagement, and improvements in surrounding environments. Dempsey's point was that conscious capitalism offered a more enlightened version of capitalism that Adam Smith, John Locke, Joseph Schumpeter, Ludwig von Mises and Milton Friedman would have appreciated and admired.

Before he dismissed his students, Dempsey told them to be prepared for his next class. He said it would be cosmic in nature. Then he casually circled back to the beginning of his lecture and mentioned that he had another reason for wearing his Baby Cakes jersey today. After leaving campus, he planned to make the 3-hour drive to Wichita to see a Wind Surge ballgame. Every kid in the class knew that he was properly dressed for the occasion.

Walking out of the lecture hall with RJ and Corey, Rachel said, "This class was eerily interesting for me. I shop at Whole Foods, I love Starbucks coffee, and I furnished my dorm at The Container Store." RJ laughed and said, "The next lecture is going to be mind-blowing. I can hardly wait." Rachel and Corey both agreed and off they all went to their next class.

CHAPTER THIRTEEN

The Age of Aquarius

SITTING AT HIS DESK IN HIS OFFICE ON CAMPUS, Professor Dempsey reviewed material for his next class. Then he checked his daily horoscope. Unlike Sarah, he believed in the uncanny accuracy of astrology and was familiar with astrological charts representing the positions of the sun, the moon, the planets, and the timing of certain events on earth. Deep in thought, Dempsey smiled thinking about the relevancy of astrology to the lecture he would deliver later that morning.

About an hour later, Dempsey walked into the lecture hall. He was wearing his Sandy Koufax Los Angeles Dodgers jersey, white with blue trim with number 32 on the front and back. Koufax pitched before Dempsey could see him on the mound in person, but, according to both his father and grandfather, he was one of the greatest pitchers of all time. In 1972, at the age of 36, Koufax became the youngest player ever to be elected into the Hall of Fame.

Standing behind the podium, Dempsey told the class that his lecture today would focus on the article in their reading material written by startup enthusiast Catherine Chan entitled "Our Transition from Age of Pisces to Aquarius: What it Means for Businesses and Meaning of Life." In this context, he asked, by a showing of hands, how many in the class followed their horoscopes and astrological signs. A few students raised their hands. Dempsey said they might find this lecture particularly illuminating. For the students who didn't raise their hands, Dempsey said that after the lecture, they might be inclined to do so.

Catherine Chan, who posted her article on the social media business website LinkedIn, believed that humanity, in astrological terms, had moved on from the Age of Pisces to enter the Age of Aquarius. She paraphrased astrologers who claimed that the Age of Aquarius paralleled major changes in the development of earth's inhabitants relating to human values, culture, society, and politics. In her view, every person on the planet had been or would be affected by this shift. In very technical terms, Chan advocated that a new astrological age occurred about every two thousand years, and this cycle affected evolution on earth.

Dempsey's lecture emphasized Catherine Chan's description of the differences between the Ages of Pisces and Aquarius. The author pointed out that the Age of Pisces was much more focused on material wealth than the Age of Aquarius. Chan prophesied that the energetic vibration on earth shifted from "earth energies," such as consumerism, material values, and hierarchies, to "air energies," including intellect, information, and collaboration. As this shift moved forward, people would become more focused on creativity and communication. Chan said "air" was the medium through which thoughts and ideas were communicated and was associated with rationality and contemplative thinking. She concluded that in this "air" Aquarian Age, there would be major advances in humanity's intellectual growth.

Paraphrasing the author, Dempsey noted that there were tendencies for the mass majority to follow bosses and religious and governmental leaders in the Age of Pisces. This behavior created top-down hierarchies. He continued that the Age of Aquarius, contrary to Piscean values, utilized bottom-up initiatives that disrupted old rules and replaced them with new ones. Through cooperation, collaboration, and community, every person would bring their gifts and skills to the table to work for the greater good. Aquarius valued innovative effort and appreciated each person's individuality. The shift away from Pisces gave rise to technological advancements, a trademark of the Aquarius Age, which produced many disruptive innovations for today and tomorrow.

Then Dempsey discussed another basic difference between the ages described in the article. He said that energy shifted into new patterns in the Age of Aquarius and old structures broke down giving way to new constructions. Contrary to the top-down approach of the Age of Pisces, the Age of Aquarius rewarded equality and partnerships. Business structure became more circular, seeking ideas from all participants in a project. Businesses operating in the Age of Aquarius practiced fairness and cooperation while those operating in the Age of Pisces produced businesses that were dominating and took control. The old ways of self-centeredness and striving for more profit and power under Pisces would no longer be the order of the day. In the Age of Aquarius, humanity would come together, collaborate, and be more interconnected.

With his technical astrological lecture complete, Dempsey pivoted and applied Catherine Chan's Age of Aquarius concept to baseball. He said to his students, "Think about a situation where Major League Baseball's political and economic system fell apart. In order to start anew, what would you do to replace it? Can you imagine a new professional baseball league that embraced both conscious capitalism and direct democracy in the Age of Aquarius? What would that league look like and how would it be structured? How would you design the league's political and ownership format? How would the economic system operate, balancing management and employees?" Dempsey asked them to ponder the concept over the weekend and be prepared at the next class to discuss their views.

The next day, after a late morning breakfast with Sarah, Dempsey drove downtown. He stopped at LaMar's Donuts on Main Street and bought a dozen. Then he spent some time at the Kansas City Urban Youth Academy before walking over to The Barber Shop to talk baseball with his friends. Dempsey entered the card shop and waved hello to Moe Franklin who was behind the counter chatting with a customer. He walked into the back room with the box of donuts in his hands. Much to his surprise, he saw Rachel, Corey, and RJ sitting around the bridge table with Frank,

Henry, and Bobby, drinking Starbucks coffee, trading baseball cards, and talking baseball.

Dempsey placed the box from LaMar's on the table and said, "Well, here are some donuts to go with your coffee." Rachel replied, "Thanks Professor Dempsey. I am glad that you're here. We were just talking about you. Your last lecture really got us thinking. Corey, RJ and I decided it would be helpful to discuss some concepts for a new professional baseball league with Moe and his friends because they love baseball, they have many more years of baseball experience than we do, and we don't think we have a monopoly on good ideas." She continued, "Preliminarily, we think our new baseball league should embrace free market economics and have a promotion and relegation system like they do in European soccer." Dempsey pulled up a chair to hear more.

Corey chimed in, "We want our new baseball league to embody many of the ideals of the Age of Aquarius. In our view, these include freedom, advanced technology, non-conformity, humanitarianism and collaboration, with a little rebellion thrown in as well." RJ added, "When we combined the ideals of the Age of Aquarius with the content of your recent lectures, it all came together for us. For example, rebellion is a theme of the Aquarius Age. Well, starting a new baseball league to compete against Major League Baseball is pretty rebellious. The political system of our new league will embrace direct democracy and use modern technology, such as mobile phones, iPads and a blockchain voting system. Our league will be non-conformist using a promotion and relegation system, a model that is not used anywhere in the United States right now." It was obvious that Dempsey was touched to see the impact his lectures had on his students. He also liked the direction their thinking was going. Then he grabbed a jelly donut from the box on the table and paused. During his moment of reflection and gratitude, the idea for a baseball-oriented class project worthy of The Age of Aquarius flashed into his mind.

CHAPTER FOURTEEN

The Field of Experimental Economics

PROFESSOR DEMPSEY WALKED INTO THE LECTURE hall for the next Political Economy class with a big smile on his face. For the first time all semester, he was not wearing a colorful baseball jersey. Instead, he wore a full-length, white laboratory coat that he borrowed from a friend who taught at the University of Kansas School of Medicine. This made him look more like a scientist than a baseball fanatic who happened to love teaching economics at the university level. Before saying a word to his students, who were no doubt stunned by his appearance, Dempsey walked back and forth across the front of the room a few times, strutting like a proud peacock to show off his new professorial attire. Dempsey milked the moment for all it was worth and, after the class shifted from astonishment to laughter, indicating their approval of his antics, he began his lecture for the day.

He said that his prepared remarks today would focus on the field of experimental economics, the application of experimental methods to study economic questions. He told the class that in the field of economics, experiments are often used to help researchers understand how and why markets and other exchange systems function as they do. By using controlled, scientific experiments, economists test choices people actually made in specific circumstances and why they did so. When done correctly under these circumstances, economic experiments captured key features of some "real world" markets and provided valuable guidance on what is likely to transpire in the future.

Dempsey said that in a typical experimental economics assessment, individual participants agree to take part in a trial and perform assigned roles such as buyers, sellers, or market competitors. The data collected during this experiment is used to test the validity of economic theories under investigation, which helps the economic researchers gain insight into market dynamics. He continued that during such an experiment, the researchers can modify the rules and the incentives to observe how doing so alters the behavior of the participants. They can also modify economic policy and observe the effects of these changes. As a part of the process, the researchers compare the actual results of the experiment with theoretical predictions previously established as to how the participants would react and respond. Using this technique in economic experiments, researchers and economists test theoretical predictions, assess the robustness of theories, and validate assumptions.

Continuing his discussion on this subject, Dempsey noted that an increasingly popular platform for testing economic experiments is agent-based computational modeling, also known as computer simulation. With this computer methodology, economists typically focus on economic processes, including dynamic system economies in which "market participants" interact with each other. In such a simulation, market participants are not actually real people. Instead, artificial intelligence is used to create computer-controlled market participants or competitors, who are programmed to behave according to the rules of the modeled system.

Then Dempsey said that he intended to expand the curriculum for the course to include an actual experiment. He told his students that they would be required to collect data, make observations, test assumptions and predictions, and would have the opportunity to interact, compete, and collaborate with fellow students. To maximize the benefits of the experiment, he challenged his students to immerse themselves in the experience, which he expected to be an exciting, collective learning lesson for everyone involved.

With many of his students now on the edge of their seats, Dempsey said, "We are going to apply the field of experimental economics to study the business of baseball. Next class, I will tell you all exactly what I have in mind for this project. It should be fun. That said, our time is up for today. Have a great weekend everyone. Oh, one last thing. Please wear your colorful baseball jerseys to our next class."

Walking out of the lecture hall together, Corey said to RJ and Rachel, "What do you think our wily Professor Dempsey has up his sleeve?" Rachel replied, "I don't know, but I can't wait to find out." RJ said, "Hey, you guys interested in going over to The Barber Shop to hang out for a bit. Rachel smiled and said, "My car is in the parking lot. Let's go! I'll drive."

CHAPTER FIFTEEN

The Class Project

FOLLOWING UP ON HIS ANTICS AT THE LAST class, Professor Dempsey swaggered into the lecture hall this time like a prized poodle groomed as a finalist in the Westminster Kennel Club Dog Show at Madison Square Garden. He was wearing an Atari video game console hoodie that he located the night before in a storage closet in the attic. Even though he hadn't seen it since graduate school, he knew exactly where Sarah had stored the hoodie, one of his college favorites.

Dempsey could see the anticipation on the faces of his students. They were waiting to hear the details of the class project he had in mind. He immediately satisfied their curiosity and said, "For our project, we are going to work together like the Founding Fathers of the United States of

America to create a new professional baseball league that will operate alongside Major League Baseball in a simulated reality. Using the highly sophisticated video game platform created by the software developers of *Out of the Park Baseball*, we will integrate the political and economic concepts we have already studied to design our league. As I said before, it should be a terrific learning experience and a lot of fun as well. So, let's get started."

Before getting into the nuts and bolts of the project, Dempsey thought it would be helpful to provide some background as to how he got this idea in the first place. He began by confessing that he had been an avid video game player since he was a teenager. He admitted that in college he had what his fraternity brothers joked was an addiction to the video game *Techmo Bowl* on Nintendo. Dempsey said that even at the University of Kansas, he was still playing video games regularly, with *SimCity,* the computer-based city planning simulation game created in 1989, being most popular in his graduate school dormitory.

Dempsey probably didn't know at that time, but *SimCity* was in many respects an experimental economic experience. A player, in the role of the city mayor, controlled the direction and economics of the game. On the outline of a blank map, the mayor could build roads, parks, bridges, and highways. He could erect office and apartment buildings, fire stations, airports, and even a baseball stadium. As time passed, the economy of the simulated city would evolve and grow, helped by the collection of taxes generating revenue and by careful budgeting and focused urban planning directed by the player. As the city continued to mature, the player could add additional buildings, such as a home for the mayor or a courthouse. He could also add to the city's infrastructure, including electricity, water, and even waste management. The residents of *SimCity*, known as "sims," were happy when the city prospered and the economy was strong. They became disgruntled if, in their view, an inappropriate decision was implemented, such as building a coal-fired power plant adjacent to their neighborhood.

While marketed as a city planning simulation game, *SimCity* provided a platform for experimenting with both political and economic systems. A player learned important economic concepts, such as supply and demand and the benefits of planning and budgeting, valuable skills for anyone to learn and master. If a player did not manage his or her city well, it could go bankrupt and its sims might move to other cities. Perhaps the most important lesson learned from *SimCity* was that everything in a society is interconnected. A decision made in one area of the society often impacted another.

SimCity was a groundbreaking video game on many levels. It became one of the most influential of its time and for decades was embraced by the educational community as an engaging video game that provided a powerful learning experience that taught useful problem-solving skills though imaginative gameplay. It also precipitated the creation of *The Sims,* a spin-off that became one of the best-selling video games of all time. In this game, a player created and controlled a virtual person, his or her own avatar. Dempsey told his students that he loved *SimCity* and *The Sims*. However, his all-time favorites were baseball simulation video games.

Those were the games he played most. With that as background, he gave the class a tutorial on those games.

According to Dempsey, the biggest leap in the evolution of baseball simulation video games occurred in 1984 when *MicroLeague Baseball* was released to be played on desktop personal computers. This was a game changer because it was one of the first video games in which the creators obtained a Major League Baseball license. This allowed the developers to feature MLB teams in games. The creators also negotiated a license with the Major League Baseball Players Association, which allowed the video game to use the likeness of actual professional ballplayers.

A *MicroLeague Baseball* player became a team's general manager, controlled the front office and the manager in the dugout, and influenced decisions made during "live" simulated games. In its original version, the game included twenty MLB teams, all selected from their glory years, such as the 1927 New York Yankees, the 1955 Brooklyn Dodgers, the 1969 New York Mets, and the 1980 Kansas City Royals. Future iterations of the software saved the results of every game and compiled statistics for every team and every player.

MicroLeague Baseball dominated the baseball simulation video game scene for more than a decade. However, as Dempsey pointed out, "creative destruction" arrived in 1999. That's when *Out of the Park Baseball*, known as *OOTP*, was released. This new video game represented a giant leap in technological innovation and made *MicroLeague Baseball* obsolete. *Out of the Park Baseball* featured the most advanced and realistic simulation engine available and incorporated modern statistical analysis. The in-game artificial intelligence produced highly realistic statistical output and tracked the most detailed and sophisticated baseball statistics. All that data was available at the fingertips of a player, together with multiple viewing and sorting options to evaluate teams and ballplayers. In addition, the game featured a database which functioned like a baseball encyclopedia retaining a complete history of statistics related to every game played.

Dempsey had set the stage with his descriptions of *SimCity* and *MicroLeague Baseball*. He followed that with the in-depth operating details of *Out of the Park Baseball*. Dempsey believed that *OOTP* had evolved with such a high level of sophistication that its technology provided the perfect platform to conduct political economy experiments for the business of baseball. Then he repeated what he had previously told his students, that the goal of the class project was for everyone to come together to create a new professional baseball league that would operate alongside Major League Baseball in a simulated reality. To accomplish this objective, he told the students that they would need to collaborate to design the political and economic model for the new league, set league and game rules, create and present a business plan for their team, and then implement their strategy as general manager to compete against the teams of their classmates. Dempsey said that they would spend the rest of the semester working on this project for a large percentage of their grade.

Dempsey then surprised the students and said, "OK everyone. Get up, pick up your belongings, and follow me.

We are going to host a constitutional congress for our new baseball league in the university food court. There, we will arrange the chairs in a big circle, like the knights of the round table, so we can better share and exchange ideas." Dempsey and the new league's "founding fathers" exited the lecture hall, walked out of the building, and made a spectacle of themselves as they marched across campus wearing the colorful baseball jerseys of their favorite ballplayers.

When Dempsey and his students walked by the window of Dean McGregor's office, McGregor heard the commotion. He put down the research paper he was reviewing and looked out of his office window to see what was going on. It was obvious from his facial expression that initially he was annoyed, displeased, and possibly even angry to see one of his professors and his students parading outside in baseball jerseys. Then his expression turned into a smile. Although he didn't particularly embrace Dempsey's teaching methods, he had to admit that the professor was very popular and got results. Many of his former students majored in economics because of him and went on to achieve success in their business careers. Several became members of the school's Alumni Association and made generous contributions to the university's annual giving program. So, the Dean turned away from the window and walked back to his desk as if he hadn't seen anything out of the ordinary.

The food court was almost empty when Dempsey and the class arrived. The students had more than enough space to form a very large circle of tables and chairs and, with the time remaining in the session, they did exactly what Dempsey had asked them to do. They discussed options and alternatives to address how to proceed in setting up their new baseball league. They agreed to spend the next two weeks, all four of the upcoming classes, doing just that. Then, they would share their recommendations with Dempsey for his review and approval.

Those two weeks went by very quickly for the students. They met officially four times during the time periods that would otherwise have been lectures, with Dempsey listening in and offering guidance when asked. The students were so motivated that almost all of them also participated in group lunches and dinners in the university food court, without Dempsey in attendance. At this point, the students believed they had successfully achieved their goal of creating what they hoped would be the perfect model for their new baseball league. They agreed that they were ready to share their conclusions with their professor.

The night before class, the students met for a special after-hours session. At evenings end, they elected Rachel president of the league, Corey its vice president, and RJ its chief technology officer. As president, Rachel was assigned the task of making the group's presentation to Professor Dempsey. As CTO, RJ was assigned the more difficult task of designing a computer application for the students to use to vote, to tabulate and retain team and individual statistical data, and to chronicle all of the league activities. RJ actually volunteered for the CTO position and he was the right student for the job. He was a true computer geek who had created several software programs while in high school and had been playing *Out of the Park Baseball* with his friends for years. The students spent the rest of the evening, way past midnight, finalizing the details of their presentation.

Dempsey dressed for class the next day just like a typical college professor. He wore khakis from Lululemon, a Banana Republic button-down shirt, and a navy-blue sports jacket that he purchased from Men's Wearhouse. He wanted the student presentation to be the focus of today's class, not one of his special baseball jerseys. When he entered the lecture hall later that day, he was surprised to see Rachel standing in his usual spot behind the podium. She said, "Professor Dempsey, if you don't mind, please take a seat." After he did, she continued, "For the last two weeks, we have had intense dialogue related to the class project you assigned to us. So, on behalf of the entire class, and as its duly elected president, I would like to present to you the principles and rules of our new baseball league." Then Rachel read from the summary that had been prepared the night before.

- The league will operate based on the principals of a constitutional republic. It will embrace a direct democracy voting system to govern. It will incorporate an economic model based on conscious capitalism.
- The league will be self-governing. It will form a judicial government with a president, a vice president, team representatives, and maintain a league court of five members to settle all disputes between teams and the league.
- The president, vice president, chief technology officer and members of the league court will serve one-year terms, with a three-year term limit. All votes will need a two-thirds majority of all members to pass.

- The league will initially have one division. Each division will consist of seventeen teams. New divisions and teams may be added as needed as the league expands in the future.
- The league will utilize a promotion and relegation system. After each season, three teams will move up and three teams will move down divisions.
- Teams will play a 162-game schedule consisting of week-long, multi-game series against each opponent.
- Each team will have a roster of 25 players and 15 players on reserve.
- Teams will be permitted to trade with each other, including players on injured reserve or on suspension.
- There will be no team salary cap, no luxury tax, and no minimum player salary.
- There will be no minor league system or affiliation.
- There will be no trade deadline.
- The rules of Major League Baseball from the 1960s will be applied. For example, there will be no designated hitter, a relief pitcher will need to face only one batter before a mound visit or a pitcher substitution, double-headers will consist of two full nine-inning games, and a runner will no longer start on second base during an extra inning game.
- With regard to league financials, there will be no visitor team gate revenue sharing, no national media contract, and each team will be able to negotiate its own local media deals.
- Team owners will have total control of their budgets. They will set pricing for tickets, merchandise, and concessions, and will be responsible for financial decisions regarding player development and scouting.

- Every player will be eligible for free agency at the end of each season, will be permitted to negotiate his or her own contract, including opt-out clauses, and will be able to sign a contract for any length, at any price, with any team.
- The player arbitration process will be abolished.
- The league will implement the "10/5 Rule" trade rule and permit veterans to veto trades.
- The Rule 5 draft will be eliminated.
- The amateur draft will be abolished.
- A new team will be permitted to join the league only at the end of each season. Just like European soccer leagues, newly admitted teams will begin play in the bottom division.
- Each team will begin with ten million dollars in the bank.

When Rachel finished her presentation, she looked at Professor Dempsey with a big smile on her face. She said that the class was open to his suggestions, and even open to suggestions from his knowledgeable friends at The Barber Shop. Dempsey believed that the students did a great job and replied that no additional input from him or anyone else would be necessary. He continued that it was now time for his students to formalize the league's constitution, develop the computer app, select their teams and players, and begin competition. Then he added, "I have taken the liberty of setting up an *Out of the Park Baseball* account for each of you. Now let's get started and have some fun." Rachel said "Not quite yet, Professor Dempsey. There's one more important issue still pending on the league's voting docket. We haven't decided on the name of our new baseball league."

Another spirited class debate began. Over the next several minutes, more than a dozen potential names for the league were considered. Then the list of possible names was whittled down to three final candidates, including the Liberty Baseball League and the United Baseball League. But with an overwhelming majority of the votes, the students agreed that the name of their new baseball league should be the Republic Baseball League.

CHAPTER SIXTEEN

The Inagural Season

After Rachel's presentation the students realized that they still had a great deal of work ahead of them to accomplish their objective. The format and rules of the league had to be codified into a formal, written constitution. A unique and interactive Republic Baseball League computer app had to be developed. Then the students needed to choose teams and begin their new "careers" as general managers of professional baseball teams using the *Out of the Park Baseball* platform. This would include signing contracts with the free-agent ballplayers they wanted on their rosters. Despite the amount of work ahead of them, the students were very excited to move forward with this new project and were looking ahead to the remaining weeks of the semester. They were also looking forward to competing against their classmates playing simulated baseball games, each hoping their team would ultimately be crowned champion of the first season of the Republic Baseball League.

Rachel and Corey shared the responsibility of drafting the Republic Baseball League Constitution. Both went online to read the most recent edition of the Official Baseball Rules, a document almost 200 pages long. They supplemented and revised these existing baseball rules with the principles and rules Rachel previously presented to Professor Dempsey in class. After a few revisions and final edits, they felt that the RBL Constitution was complete. They emailed a PDF copy to Dempsey who gave it his stamp of approval the next day.

At the same time that Rachel and Corey were hard at work on the RBL's governing document, RJ spent the night sitting at his desk in front of his computer in his dorm developing an app for his iPhone, other mobile phones, iPads, and laptops. Given his experience with software programming, he was able to complete the task doing an all-nighter, taking breaks only for coffee. The app had all of the usual bells and whistles, such as user name, password, communication capabilities, including texting, and a search engine. The app also included a section that permitted users to cast votes, to import, tabulate and retain team and individual statistical data, and to chronicle activities related to their teams. After some testing, RJ was certain that the app was ready for RBL participants to use.

In preparation for his next class, Professor Dempsey wore the St. Louis Cardinals jersey of ex-ballplayer and major league manager, Tony LaRussa. This was a symbolic gesture on his part because LaRussa was one on the greatest baseball managers of all time. With almost 3,000 managerial wins under his belt for three different teams, he trailed only the legendary Connie Mack for most wins all-time. Now, each of Dempsey's students would manage a ballclub in the Republic Baseball League, just like Tony LaRussa. Coincidentally, Dempsey also knew that LaRussa made his major league debut in 1963 playing for the Kansas City Athletics, not far from his boyhood home in Wichita and a short distance from the UMKC campus where he taught economics.

Dempsey chose not to lecture on economics during this class. Instead, he asked the students to report on the progress they had made on the class project. Rachel and Corey reported that the Republic Baseball League Constitution was completed and reviewed. RJ reported that the RBL app was developed and ready to go. Then Dempsey asked what the students planned to do next. Rachel raised her hand and said, "We are way ahead of you Professor Dempsey. Tonight, all of us are meeting in the food court at 7pm. We are bringing our mobile phones and computers so that we can get familiar with the RBL app, then pick our teams, and select our players. I expect it to be a marathon session and you are welcome to join us if you like." Dempsey responded, "Thank you for the invitation but I've got some more PhD thesis research to do this evening, and I'm on a roll. But I'll be there in spirit. Have fun tonight everyone."

Anxious to get started, most of the students in the class were already in the food court when Rachel, Corey and RJ arrived ten minutes before 7pm. RJ needed only a few minutes to demonstrate the Republic Baseball League app on his iPhone because every student in the class was already computer savvy and caught on quickly. Then he reviewed the *Out of the Park Baseball* video game software and again the students caught on without a hitch.

After that, each student, in alphabetical order, picked their independent baseball teams. Rachel chose the Grand Junction Rockies, Corey selected the Chicago Dogs, and RJ decided to become the general manager of the Lincoln Saltdogs. Then the students began the tasks of selecting baseball players for their team rosters. The 7-hour marathon session finally ended after the last ballplayer "signed" his contract. Despite the fact that everyone was pumped up and anxious to start playing simulated baseball games, Corey suggested that they all go back to their dorms, sleep for a few hours, and get ready for classes the next day. That's exactly what they all did.

For the weeks remaining in the fall semester, Dempsey's students played simulated Republic Baseball League games against their classmates. Ballgames were played at various times throughout the day, before class, in between classes, and after classes, often starting as early as 9am and ending at midnight. Several games could be played and finished in a short period of time because each game was simulated automatically by the *OOTP* software engine. Each student, fulfilling his or her role as general manager, made all of the back office and on-the-field decisions for the team, and looked to be really enjoying their participation in the class project.

As part of the process, students initially communicated with each other via text messaging and phone calls to discuss trades. However, after a few days, most of the students agreed to meet up in the food court at night to play games face-to-face, to watch each other's games, and to talk trades. It was a lively, friendly, somewhat noisy environment and it was attracting interest from other students dining in the food court who were interested in knowing what was going on.

Given the level of excitement, Corey decided to set up a Twitch account, a live, interactive streaming video service owned by a subsidiary of Amazon. This account allowed him to broadcast simulated RBL games as they were being played. Every Friday night for the rest of the semester, Corey walked around the food court with a GoPro video camera in hand to record all of the action taking place around the league. He even posted interviews with team general managers throughout the evening. Corey labeled the account, not surprisingly, "The Republic Baseball League."

The excitement surrounding the class project was not limited to the food court. A buzz started to grow around campus as well. Corey's Twitch account was gaining dozens of new UMKC followers every day. The buzz extended to friends and family of Dempsey's students as well as to students at other colleges.

Perhaps with an eye to a future career in sports broadcasting, Corey was inspired to launch a daily video recap show on YouTube entitled *RBL Today,* similar to ESPN's *SportsCenter.* He intended to use this platform to dish out box scores of the day's games and to share league news on a daily basis. Corey was able to do this by taking full advantage of another creative and unique feature of the *Out of the Park Baseball* platform. In addition to reporting simulated game details, accumulating and storing enormous amounts of statistical information, and permitting interactivity between general managers, the video game generated a wide variety of fictional news articles and communications on the fly. With this feature, video game players expected to hear about a slugger pounding four homers in a game or a pitcher tossing a no-hitter.

Ballplayers, managers, and coaches operating inside *OOTP* were not just about wins and losses, ratings and stats. They were given personalities. They were just like "the sims." The video game software produced interesting and often unusual personal interest stories about its fictional baseball players. In fact, Corey told one of these stories during his first *RBL Today* broadcast. He reported the "breaking news" that Justin Watts, a pitcher on the roster of the Southern Illinois Miners, a ballclub selected by another Dempsey student, set off fireworks in his backyard and suffered a freak injury. According to Corey, team officials did not disclose the nature of the injury sustained but said Watts would be out of action for the next two months of the season. Video game "reporters" speculated on what Watts may have done to upset the Baseball Gods.

The next day, Corey posted another personal interest story that crossed the Republic Baseball League newswire. This narrative did not even involve baseball. It was about music. The headline read, "Marc Wangenstein Releases Swing Album." According to the press release, when not playing the outfield for the Lexington Legends in Kentucky, Wangenstein could usually be found singing with his swing band in his hometown of Ronkonkoma, New York. When asked about the origins of the band, Wangenstein was quoted saying, "We first got together when we were in high school. Last summer, when we were on stage at a local fair, a music producer saw us playing. He asked if we were interested in signing a contract with him and recording an album. Of course, we said yes. While music may not be as steady as baseball, it's definitely a good thing to have as an option after retirement."

Wangenstein was not the only RBL ballplayer working on a side gig. In his third *RBL Today* broadcast, Corey featured Ricky Ramirez Jr., left fielder for Florence Y'alls, another RBL team located in Kentucky. This personal interest story told the tale of Ramirez opening up a CrossFit Gym. The outfielder came to spring training in great shape, the best shape of his career. When coaches and teammates asked him how he did it, he told them that it was the result of dedicated CrossFit training in the offseason. He said that he became so enamored with this style of fitness that he opened his own CrossFit franchise in his hometown of Marysville, California. "I want to pass on my love for this type of fitness training to others," he said. "I'm obviously not going to be able to be at the facility that often during the season but I'll stop by whenever I can and I'll definitely be there all of the time in the offseason. Who knows. Maybe I'll open up a chain of CrossFit training centers after I retire from baseball." Ramirez clearly had put in the hard work off the field at the gym during the offseason. Now he had the chance to show off its benefits on the baseball diamond.

In his next *RBL Today* broadcast, Corey paid homage to "Opening Day," that special day of the year that signifies the start of every baseball season. Corey made a video selfie and said, "Opening day is a time of joy and optimism for all baseball fans. It's a time for families to bond around America's favorite pastime, to get away from the real world for three to four hours, to enjoy a few hot dogs, hamburgers, peanuts, and a beer, to holler at the umpires, and to cheer their favorite team to victory. Baseball's call to action, 'Play Ball,' can be heard all across the country just before the first pitch of baseball season is thrown. The Republic Baseball League begins this week in what promises to be an incredible year of baseball." To make sure this video received as much exposure as possible, Corey posted it on both his Twitch and Twitter accounts. These posts received hundreds of "likes."

Dempsey continued to lecture his students on basic political and economic concepts for the remainder of the semester. However, he made sure to reserve the last few minutes of each class to discuss the status of the class project. He was very pleased with its progress. The students were taking their Republic Baseball League general manager responsibilities seriously. Trades and roster changes were being made and the rules of the RBL Constitution were being followed. At the end of each class, Rachel, as league president, presented the current league standings.

During these last few weeks of the semester, Dempsey was busy doing additional research on his PhD thesis. He had made so much progress that he even completed a first draft of his dissertation. He realized, however, that his concentration on this project prevented him from spending as much quality time as he would have liked hanging out with his friends down at The Barber Shop. So, he set aside the next Saturday afternoon to do just that. He drove downtown, picked up a slab of ribs from Arthur Bryant's barbecue joint on his way, and entered the doorway of the back room of the baseball card shop. To his surprise, Moe, Frank, Bobby, and Henry were not playing cards. Nor were they talking about Major League Baseball. They were sitting around the bridge table staring at their iPhones watching Corey Gordon on *RBL Today*. Dempsey stood in the doorway, holding the tray of barbeque ribs, in disbelief. Then he heard Moe say to Frank, "Hey, the first season of the Republic Baseball League is almost over. If Gordon's Chicago Dogs win, I believe you'll owe me fifty bucks." Dempsey could not believe what he was witnessing. Then he said, "Hi fellas, how about some ribs." They continued to discuss the RBL until the last rib was gone.

Given the amount of time they spent together, Rachel, Corey, and RJ were becoming best friends. They were also falling in love with baseball, specifically with the business of baseball. Each had been pursuing different college majors before taking Professor Dempsey's class, but now they discussed taking courses that would prepare them for careers related to the business of baseball. So, in preparation for the spring semester, they agreed to register for Statistics 101 and Introduction to Sports Management. The trio also started new traditions. After class, they would regularly travel to The Barber Shop to study, drink coffee, and talk baseball in the back room with Moe Franklin and his friends. On weekends, when they weren't studying or playing simulated RBL baseball games, they got together as often as possible to attend Kansas City Monarchs ball-games at Legends Field in Kansas City, Kansas.

During the last week of the semester, Corey somehow found the time to launch *The Business of Baseball* on RBL's YouTube channel. It was a weekly broadcast that covered all things financial and business-related in the league. In the initial episode, he summarized the RBL season to date noting that RJ's Lincoln Saltdogs, currently in first place, were likely to be the winners of the league's first season. As to the business of baseball, he emphasized that each team in the league, except one, was successful. Every organization, other than the Monterey Amberjacks, earned a profit in their first year in business. Clearly, Dempsey's students, acting as general managers, were running their ballclubs very efficiently.

For the next to last class of the fall semester, Dempsey asked his students to wear baseball jerseys again. They all complied. Having given it thought the night before, he wore his Lou Gehrig jersey again, in memory of his grandfather. Standing behind his desk, he called Rachel to the front of the lecture hall and asked her to report on the status of the class project. Without hesitation, she said what everyone already knew. The first season of the Republic Baseball League was indeed a big success. RJ's Lincoln Saltdogs did retain their lead and emerged as league champions with a record of 105 wins and only 57 losses. Rachel turned to face her professor and said, "Most importantly, all of us have learned a great deal about politics and economics in your class, Professor Dempsey, and, because of you, we had fun doing it. Thank you very much!"

An emotional Dempsey walked over to the podium and responded, "Thank you very much, Rachel, for those kind words." He turned to the class and continued, "And thank you all for making this such a great semester for me. I hope you know a lot more about the political economy now than you did before you registered for this class. And I'd like to congratulate you all on successfully completing the class project. Your final grades will certainly reflect the great work all of you did."

Then Dempsey invited RJ to come up to the front of the lecture hall to receive the Republic Baseball League championship trophy that the professor had purchased from The Barber Shop. Dempsey said, "Congratulations, RJ. Your Lincoln Saltdogs are the first champions of the Republic Baseball League." RJ hoisted the trophy over his head as his fellow classmates cheered and gave him a standing ovation. To wrap up the semester, Dempsey handed each of his students a take-home final exam, due on or before the last class of the semester.

As a final gesture to celebrate the completion of the first season of the Republic Baseball League, the students threw a baseball-themed party in the food court. Everyone had a great time, especially Dempsey, a very proud economics professor who was designated by the students as the guest of honor.

CHAPTER SEVENTEEN

The Thesis

PROFESSOR DEMPSEY WAS SITTING IN HIS university office with an early morning cup of coffee on the right-hand corner of his desk. He reflected back several months ago when the idea for a baseball-related class project, worthy of the Age of Aquarius and his PhD thesis, first flashed into his mind in the back room of The Barber Shop. Dempsey knew that in order for his analytical thesis to carry sufficient weight for a PhD dissertation, he needed to use the scientific method to accomplish his objective. He was aware that this empirical method of questioning and confirming scientific knowledge, which had been practiced for decades, typically involved careful observation, rigorous questioning, skepticism of what is observed, formulating hypotheses, experimenting and testing the hypotheses, analyzing data, and reporting a conclusion. The process was designed to help scientists and researchers discover cause and effect relationships by carefully gathering and examining data and evidence to ascertain if all of the available information could be combined into logical conclusions. These concepts began to infiltrate Dempsey's mind and he spent the next few hours typing his thoughts into a Word document on his laptop computer.

Experiment: The Republic Baseball League

Ask Question(s): Is Major League Baseball's antitrust exemption good for the game of baseball? Is the exemption in the best interests of its consumers, its baseball fans? Is the exemption in the best interests of the overall United States economy? Is the exemption in the best interest of American society? Does the exemption stifle competition and infringe upon other market participants, including independent baseball leagues, affiliated minor league baseball teams, minor league baseball players, and even its consumers? What would be the impact to the United States economy and all of the market participants if Congress removed baseball's antitrust protection?

Form a Hypothesis: The U.S. economy and American society would benefit if Congress, or the courts through the judicial process, removed Major League Baseball's antitrust exemption. New professional baseball leagues, such as the Republic Baseball League, would not threaten the profitability of MLB or its team owners. An experiment will combine the extensive volume of data currently available with additional data to be produced to prove this point. The experiment will demonstrate that by allowing the baseball economy to operate freely after MLB's antitrust exemption is removed, both baseball and the overall economy of the U.S. will grow exponentially benefitting all of the market participants.

Implement the Experiment: Create a new professional baseball league modeled after the Republic Baseball League. Use simulation software, such as *Out of the Park Baseball*, to replicate real professional baseball. The new league will be formed selecting its players and coaches from the 120 minor league teams in Major League Baseball's affiliate system. To insure accuracy and reliability of the data and evidence produced, the experiment will simulate five full baseball league seasons.

Analyze Data: From a macroeconomic perspective, the analysis will study and evaluate multiple business trends generated by the league, such as season ticket sales, game attendance, media sales, merchandise sales, gate revenue, team payroll, total revenue, and total expenses. From a microeconomic perspective, analysis will study and examine whether former minor league teams and the baseball players on their rosters are better off financially after joining the Republic Baseball League. The analysis will also study and evaluate whether the new league's existence will have an adverse impact on Major League Baseball.

Formulate a Conclusion: The experiment will test its thesis and conclude that the rise of the Republic Baseball

League is beneficial to a much broader group of baseball players and is not a competitive threat to Major League Baseball's hegemony. The success of the Republic Baseball League will demonstrate that when the professional baseball market is allowed to operate freely, the financial results are beneficial to all participants. As a result, the experiment will conclude that United States Congress should indeed act decisively to pass legislation to revoke MLB's antitrust exemption.

Dempsey was so absorbed in his thinking that he didn't realize that he had been working at his computer for more than four hours. With his first summary draft completed, he stood up, stretched, and decided to take a break and get something to eat. When he arrived at the university café, he smiled seeing many of his students sitting at tables talking about the success of the Republic Baseball League. He just knew he was on the right track with his thesis. When he returned to his office after lunch, he reread the draft and made several edits to the document. With another economics class to teach that afternoon, he saved the draft and then turned off his computer.

The professor was back at his desk early the next morning. He opened the Word document and read the summary again. He was pleased with it, so much so that he printed it, put it in a manila folder, and walked briskly down the hallway to Dean McGregor's office. Dempsey knocked on the Dean's door, was invited in, and took the seat offered to him in front of the Dean's desk. Dempsey, with an anxious look on his face, handed the Dean the summary describing the scientific method he planned to use in his PhD thesis.

With a warm cup of Quik Trip coffee in his hand, Dean McGregor took his time and slowly read Dempsey's summary with discernment. Then he lifted his eyes, looked straight at Dempsey, and said, "Congratulations, Kevin. You've got yourself the beginnings of what I hope will be an excellent, insightful PhD thesis." With a rarely seen smile on his face, he continued, "You are certainly heading in the right direction. Now get to work and finish it." That's exactly what Dempsey planned to do.

CHAPTER EIGHTEEN

The Dissertation

AFTER HIS BRIEF, ENCOURAGING MEETING WITH Dean McGregor, Professor Dempsey walked back to his office, put on his Kansas City Monarchs jersey, pulled down the shades to darken the room, turned on the blue, white, and red Kansas Jayhawk lamp on his desk, and called Sarah to give her his good news. Then he opened his laptop and went to the university website to schedule an appointment to present his PhD dissertation to the Dean and other tenured members of the economics department. With a few more clicks, he entered the required information and confirmed the appointment.

Dempsey took a deep breath and clicked on the *OOTP 22* icon on his computer screen. After the software loaded, he clicked "Create a new league" and then selected the option to "Customize your league." He recreated the class project baseball simulation league with a few adjustments. The minimum wage was set at $35,000 per year for baseball players. The scheduling algorithm was also tweaked to ensure that teams would only play teams from within their own division. Divisions were also expanded from 17 to 30 teams. The league was formed with 120 teams from Major League Baseball's minor league affiliate system. Team rosters were liquidated and all the baseball players and coaches became free agents, a critical element of Dempsey's free market approach to baseball economics.

Dempsey clicked the simulation button and watched with excitement as the computer algorithms worked their magic. Dempsey felt like a young boy on Christmas morning as he looked over all of the data produced during the first year of the simulation. He had seen the software program do this hundreds of times before, but this time it was different. This was his new league in action, with updated rules and protocol, setting the table for his PhD thesis and dissertation. He watched excitedly as the software, with lightning speed, began to run through each of the five years of seasonal play Dempsey had programmed it to do.

Dempsey took a break from his computer, left his office, and headed to the café. Deep in thought, while sipping hot coffee, he realized that all of the many hours he spent on the third floor of the university library researching baseball economic history was time well spent. So much of the material he accumulated would find its way into his thesis. Dempsey returned to his office and reviewed the volume of data produced from the simulation.

Dempsey devoted the next few days analyzing the data more carefully in greater detail. At the end of the first fiscal year, many teams in the simulation earned a profit. Now with more cash to spend and better predictability about future revenue streams in areas such as media rights, season tickets, and merchandise sales, the teams around the league began to offer higher salaries and larger contracts, which attracted Major League Baseball veteran players. Carlos Rodon, Jake Arrieta, Wade Miley, and Brandon Belt were the well-known baseball players who joined a Republic Baseball League Division 1 team for the 2022 season. Division 2 had even more Major League Baseball veterans join teams, including Alex Cobb, Michael A. Taylor, Marwin Gonzalez, Josh Harrison, Matt Carpenter, Matt Harvey, Starlin Castro and Jonathan Villar. Familiar MLB names that joined RBL Division 3 teams included Matt Wieters, Edinson Volquez, Dexter Fowler, Seth Lugo, and Adam Eaton. Even Division 4 teams were able to sign veteran MLB players such as Josh Reddick and Dee Strange-Gordon.

As Dempsey expected, team payrolls increased dramatically from 2021 to 2022, but so did team revenues. More Republic Baseball League teams earned an annual profit in 2022 and by the end of 2023, every team in the league was profitable. The profits were not just enjoyed by the team owners. The baseball players benefitted as well. The average player salary in 2023 was $120,000. Many of these baseball players were playing in the former MLB minor leagues earning at most $15,000 per season.

According to the feedback reported by the *OOTP* software, the fans were also sharing in the success of the Republic Baseball League. Attendance around the league was robust and most teams consistently played in front of large crowds. The fans enjoyed higher quality baseball on the field each season while ticket prices remained low and extremely affordable for a typical family of four to attend a game. The promotion and relegation system also proved to be critical to the league's success as even teams way down in the division standings still had a reason to fight hard until the end of the season. As a result, the fans remained engaged for all 162 games.

Dempsey's *OOTP* experiment proved to be a great success. Major League Baseball teams continued to enjoy multi-million-dollar television contracts and their thirty teams continued to pay multi-million-dollar salaries to their top players. Top prospects such as Bobby Witt, Jr. remained in Major League Baseball and top college prospects, such as Robert Moore, were drafted by MLB teams and signed contracts. The Republic Baseball League proved to be a healthy economic counterbalance, rather than a threat, to Major League Baseball. Dempsey felt equally certain that Dean MacGregor and his contemporaries in the Economics Department would reach the same conclusion.

Dempsey had previously spent months researching material and drafting sections for his thesis. So, all he had left to complete the paper was to add recently accumulated comparative data from the five-year RBL simulation. This didn't take him very long and he was pleased with the final product. He reread his dissertation one last time, from beginning to end, and felt completely satisfied that it was ready for submission. All that remained on his long road to his PhD in Economics was his oral presentation.

Dempsey spent two days practicing, pretending he was

speaking in front of the PhD review board. First, he practiced silently to himself. Then he practiced out loud. Then he practiced in front of a mirror. Finally, he practiced in front of Sarah, who made a few suggestions and offered some good advice. Given all of this practice, and the quality of his thesis, Dempsey was confident that his oral presentation in front of the Dean and economics department professors would go well.

Dempsey arrived early on campus for his big day. Although confident, he was still a little anxious as he walked from his office to the large classroom where he would give his oral presentation. When he entered the room, he saw a copy of his thesis on the desk. He said, "Thank you all for coming to my PhD dissertation today. I hope you find my presentation interesting and captivating, and that you conclude that it breaks new ground related to politics, economics and the business of baseball." For the next hour, Dempsey made his case and presented data and comparative analysis he accumulated from his experiment.

To conclude his presentation, Dempsey made these closing remarks, "Major League Baseball is broken. It has been broken for a very long time. The thirty MLB teams continue to earn millions in profits annually and franchise values continue to increase. Yet the fan experience continues to decline, the cost to attend a ballgame continues to increase, and hundreds of minor league baseball players are still getting paid an annual salary below the poverty line. These problems persist because Major League Baseball continues to enjoy its antitrust exemption. With congressional and Supreme Court protection, Major League Baseball operates like an authoritarian, communist government that embraces an economic model akin to a monopolistic oligopoly. This oligarchy conspires to squeeze the minor league baseball players to maximize profits. Enough is enough. The time has come for change. Positive change. Evolutionary change. Professional baseball needs to get back to its original American values and dig its roots in deep so that the business of baseball once again embodies the spirit of libertarianism that was in the hearts of our American Founding Fathers. To quote a phrase, 'as goes baseball, so goes the United States of America, and as goes the United States of America, so goes the world.' May current and future generations in this great country continue to fulfill the promise of the American dream and may each citizen, and every immigrant that arrives to this land, enjoy life, liberty, property, the pursuit of happiness, and professional baseball without its antitrust exemption. May God bless America and may the Baseball Gods bless the Republic Baseball League. Thank you very much."

CHAPTER NINETEEN

The Golden Age

BACK IN HIS OFFICE AFTER HIS DISSERTATION presentation, Professor Dempsey felt completely exhausted. Despite hours of intensive preparation and a high level of confidence, he still found the experience both stressful and demanding. He decided a few minutes of meditation would be helpful and he was right. Feeling more relaxed afterwards, he called Sarah to give her the news that the presentation went well and all that was standing between him and his PhD was the acceptance of his thesis and dissertation, and, of course, the stamp of approval from the review board.

After chatting on the telephone with Sarah, Dempsey spent some time preparing for his last lecture of the semester. He was just about finished when he was interrupted by a knock on his office door. He said, "Enter" and in walked Rachel, Corey, and RJ. Rachel said, "We know you are not a PhD just yet, but in anticipation of you earning that advanced degree, our class decided to chip in and buy you a congratulations gift. They designated the three of us to deliver it to you." RJ said, "Taking your class this semester was truly amazing, it changed our lives. Everyone in the class feels the same way. We are forever grateful to you." Then Corey handed Dempsey a package neatly wrapped in red, white, and blue giftwrap paper and said, "Thank you for everything."

Dempsey carefully removed the giftwrap paper from the package. It was a shoebox. He opened it an inch, peeked inside, and what he saw in it put a big smile on his face. The shoebox was filled with unopened packs of baseball cards from the 1970s. Since the cards were still in their original packaging, Dempsey knew that they were in mint condition and no doubt worth a pretty penny. Humbled by the considerate gift, Dempsey said, "You guys shouldn't have done this. It was totally unnecessary. This is so thoughtful of you and I truly appreciate it. You guys are amazing, and I will remember this forever." Dempsey placed the shoebox on his desk and said, "Come with me. It's time for you to hear my last lecture of the semester. I think you will appreciate the subject matter." Then he changed his mind and took the shoebox with him to the lecture hall.

Rachel, Corey, and RJ walked with Dempsey down the hallway. When they entered the lecture hall, Dempsey saw his students already in their seats. Appropriate for the occasion, they all were wearing the baseball jerseys of their favorite Republic Baseball League teams. Rachel, Corey, and RJ walked to the top row, found seats, and sat down.

Dempsey walked over to the podium carrying the shoebox and said, "I guess you all know what I'm holding and what's inside. This was so thoughtful of all of you and I can't thank you enough. Your gift is right on the mark for a fanatic baseball fan like me, but I guess you knew that too. Thanks again from the bottom of my heart." Dempsey was overcome with emotion and his students could see his eyes actually tearing up a little.

Feeling the good vibes, Dempsey opened his laptop and said, "Now let's get down to the business at hand." He located his class presentation folder and clicked on the file entitled "The Golden Age." Dempsey channeled his inner Socrates and began his lecture telling his students that Webster's dictionary defines the term "Golden Age" as a period of great happiness, prosperity and achievement. Similarly, Oxford Languages defines the term as a past time of peace, prosperity, and happiness and adds that it could define a period when a specific art, skill, or activity is at its peak. According to Wikipedia, the term comes from Greek mythology and denotes a time of peace, harmony, stability and prosperity when great tasks are accomplished.

Then Dempsey referenced Mark Twain to illustrate that golden ages come and go, and come back again, although not exactly in the same form in a different time. Twain once said that "History does not repeat itself, but it rhymes." Dempsey believed Twain was right, even if he failed to mention in any of his writings that time may not be linear, but rather a spiral or circular in nature. Dempsey compared the concept to a wedding ring where there is no beginning and no end.

Dempsey then used another analogy to make his point. He noted that the world has been in peril many, many times throughout history. Humanity has faced wars, pandemics, economic disparity, racial injustice, tyrannical governments, and even genocide. Yet, these tragic events, be they moments in time or situations that last for much longer periods of time, are often birthing pains of the next golden age. Dempsey's research on the topic revealed that historians have used the phrase "Golden Age" to describe events and accomplishments that span different cultures and time frames. These include Ancient Greece of Plato and Aristotle, the Italian Renaissance of Michelangelo and Leonardo di Vinci, the Scientific Revolution of Copernicus and Isaac Newton, the Age of Enlightenment of John Locke and Adam Smith, and the Industrial Revolution in the United States of America with Henry Ford and Andrew Carnegie.

Although clearly not in the same realm as war, pandemics or tyrannical governments, or nearly as important as the cultural, scientific, or industrial advancements of the golden ages he had just outlined, Dempsey chose to devote the last segment of his last lecture of the semester to describe the golden age of baseball. According to the professor, many baseball historians believe that the first golden age of baseball began in the 1920s, after the dead-ball era before World War I, and lasted until the 1940s and World War II. This period was dominated by the New York Yankees, especially the great Lou Gehrig and the incomparable home run hitting Babe Ruth. Other baseball historians believe that this golden age of baseball extended further, after World War II through the 1960s. This period was noted for the expansion of baseball to the west coast, the Dodgers to Los Angeles and the Giants to San Francisco, the invention of color television, and the outstanding careers and charisma of modern era baseball legends like Willie Mays, Mickey Mantle, Sandy Koufax and Bob Gibson.

Dempsey continued, "Our class project gave us all a glimpse into the possible future of professional baseball and its next golden age. Together, we reimagined what baseball in this great country of ours could be if Major League Baseball's monopolistic antitrust exemption was revoked. We would see a bright future, a bright future indeed, with every person and every business connected in some way to baseball benefitting. Ballplayers would benefit, especially the ranks of those that toil currently in the minor leagues. Owners would benefit as the value of their franchises would continue to increase in value. Perhaps most important, the fans would benefit by having greater access to quality baseball at a reasonable price closer to home."

To complete his lecture and the last class, Dempsey said, "Thank you all for taking my class this semester. I hope you learned a great deal about politics and economics and had some fun doing it. And thank you for your enthusiasm and participation in our class project, which led me to my PhD thesis and dissertation. May the Baseball Gods always be with you and long live the Republic Baseball League."

CHAPTER TWENTY

The PhD

PROFESSOR DEMPSEY WAS ON PINS AND NEEDLES waiting to hear from Dean MacGregor with what he hoped would be good news. He passed the time by researching material for his economics classes for the upcoming semester, updating related curriculum, and spending several afternoons downtown at the Kansas City Urban Youth Baseball Academy working with the kids. He also spent more time at The Barber Shop to talk baseball with his buddies.

On baseball card poker night, Dempsey entered the back room carrying the shoebox. He opened it, placed the packs of baseball cards on the bridge table, and said, "I brought these extra special baseball cards for our poker game tonight. They were a gift from my Political Economy class, hand delivered to me in my office by Rachel, Corey, and RJ."

Dempsey didn't realize that Moe already knew about this gift and the contents of the shoebox. Rachel, Corey and RJ had visited his shop the week before to purchase the baseball cards for their professor. Moe, pretending to look surprised at the cards on the table said, "Oh, man. You got yourself some baseball cards from the dark ages there. I'm not sure if you're old enough to know all of these ballplayers." Dempsey laughed at Moe's joke, handed out the packs, and sat down at the table to play some baseball card poker.

Thirty minutes later, after trading cards with each other, Moe said, "I got a royal flush!" He laid down the baseball cards for Amos Otis, Cookie Rojas, Buck Martinez, Steve Busby, and Frank White, who all played for the Kansas City Royals in the 1970s. Bobby replied, "Darn it. I was one card away from a full house."

When the poker game ended, Dempsey started to pick up the baseball cards on the bridge table and place them back in the shoebox. Before he finished, his iPhone rang. He stopped picking up cards, took his phone out of his pocket, and checked to see who was calling. The call was from Dean McGregor, and Dempsey's heart skipped a beat.

With an anxious look on his face, Dempsey swiped his phone with his index finger and answered the call. Dean McGregor said, "Hello Kevin, so sorry to bother you at this late hour but I have some important news to share with you and I felt it simply could not wait until Monday. Congratulations, Professor Dempsey, you are now a PhD in Economics. You passed with flying colors. You will be glad to know that the vote was unanimous. Everyone agreed that your thesis was very well-written, thoughtful, and provocative and your dissertation presentation was excellent. We all agreed with your conclusion as well." Dempsey thanked the Dean and told him that earning his PhD in Economics was a dream come true.

Immediately after he disconnected the phone call, Dempsey made a prayer gesture with his hands, looked up to the heavens, and said to himself, "Baseball Gods, I thank you." Then he told Moe, Henry, Frank, and Bobby the good news and they congratulated him. Moe got up from his chair, gave Dempsey a big hug, and said, "You worked long and hard, man. You deserve this. You earned your PhD!" Then Henry, Frank, and Bobby stood up and each gave Dempsey a hug.

Dempsey sent a group text to Rachel, Corey, and RJ thanking them again for their thoughtful gift and telling them his good news. Rachel immediately replied, "Congrats Professor Dempsey, we knew you would do it!" Corey quickly responded with, "Congratulations on becoming a PhD! Great news!" RJ responded with, "Let's go! Congrats Professor Dempsey!"

Saving the best for last, Dempsey called Sarah with the good news. She literally screamed with joy at his good fortune and said, "I'm so proud and happy for you! Congratulations sweetheart." Feeling a sense of accomplishment and humble pride, Dempsey told Sarah that he would be forever grateful for — The Republic Baseball League.

THE ACKNOWLEDGEMENTS

To Reggie Fink, The Soulmate

To Kayla Fink, The College Student

To Nate Fink, The High School Baseball Player

To Beth and Jeffrey Fink, The Supportive Parents

To Meg Schader, The Editor

To Meg Reid, The Book Cover and Book Layout Designer

To Out of the Park Baseball, The Simulation Software

To Catherine Chan, The Age of Aquarius

To Daniel Gallen, The Sportswriter

To John Mackey and Professor Raj Sisodia,

To Adam Smith, John Locke, Thomas Jefferson, Ludwig von Mises, Patrick Henry, Lemuel Haynes, Milton Friedman, and Joseph Schumpeter, The Political Economists

To John Mackey and Professor Sisodia,
The Conscious Capitalists

To Jon Perrin, The Apprentice

Kevin Dempsey @Dempsey_... · 5/21/22 ···

I played ball for Wichita State in the 80's. Still love coming to games. Fun watching the Shockers sweep Tulane last weekend. 🧹

99 views

2

Kevin Dempsey @Dempsey_... · 5/21/22 ···

Tulane Baseball has a terrific dugout culture. Despite recent slump due to a ton of injuries, they have a bright future ahead. Roll wave! 🌊 @GreenWaveBSB

229 views

1 7

Kevin Dempsey @Dempsey_... · 5/21/22 ···

Ted Lasso, you inspired this Twitter account. Much respect and gratitude!

@TedLasso @RBL___ @scooterfink

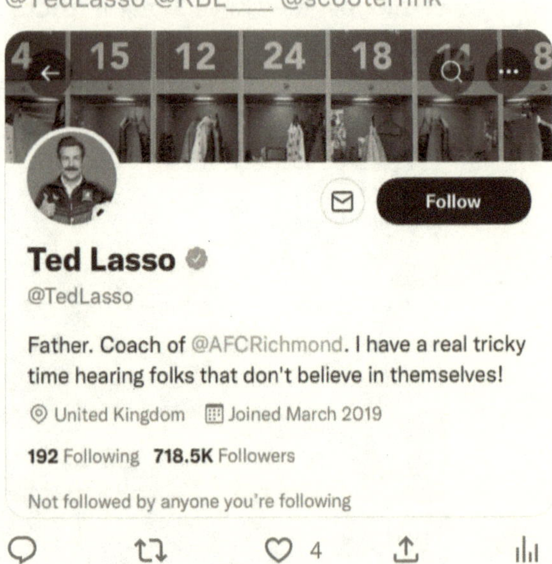

Kevin Dempsey @Dempsey_... · 5/21/22 ···
Been obsessed with collective baseball cards since I was a child...

2

Kevin Dempsey @Dempsey_... · 5/22/22 ···

Baseball is nothing more than another classroom in the educational process. Really, baseball is a metaphor for life. -Augie Garrido

6

Kevin Dempsey @Dempsey_... · 5/23/22 ···

What happened yesterday is over, today is the first day of the rest of your life! 🌻

9

Kevin Dempsey @Dempsey_... · 5/23/22 ···
Been watching a lot of high school baseball lately. State championships this week. Wichita State hosting 5A. My prediction for winner? - Blue Valley Southwest
@_benbybee @BVSW_BSB

6

Kevin Dempsey @Dempsey_... · 5/23/22 ···
I'd rather be at a baseball game, but my wife Sarah prefers museums. Happy wife, happy life. 🎨

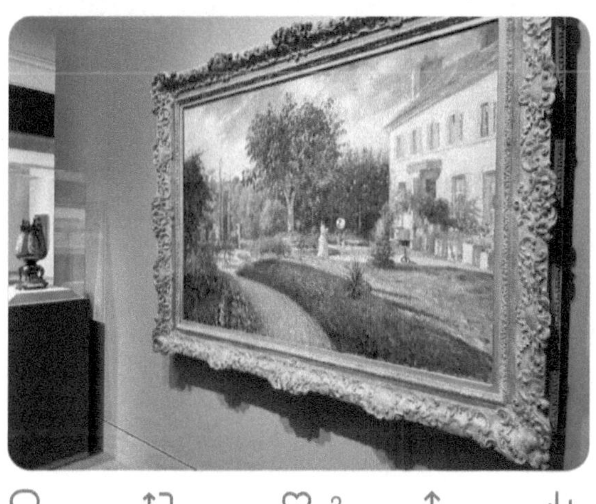

2

Kevin Dempsey @Dempsey_... · 5/23/22 ···
Excited to check out this book! 📚
@TheSavBananas @YellowTuxJesse

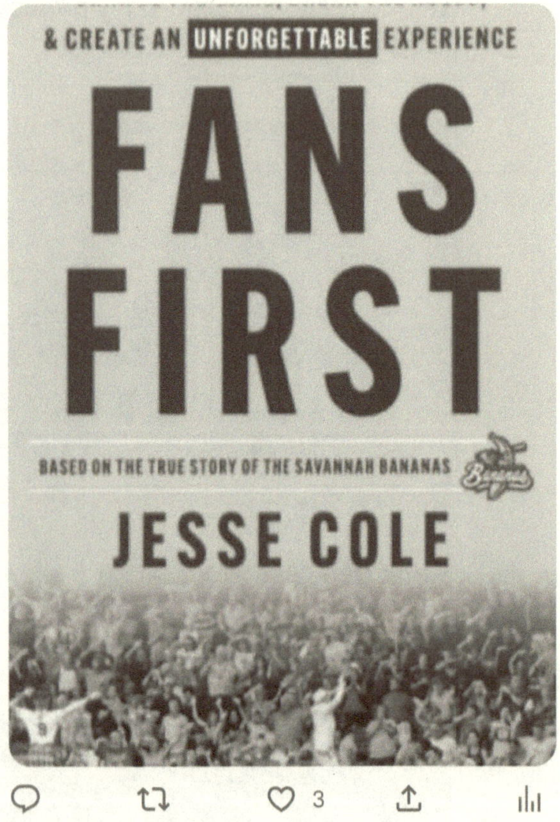

3

Kevin Dempsey @Dempsey_... · 5/27/22 ···

Eye Silver. Never seen that before! ⚾

2

Kevin Dempsey @Dempsey_... · 5/27/22 ···
My prediction has come to pass. Blue Valley Southwest has won back to back Kansas 5A state championships. Team effort. Ben Bybee, Cooper Kelly, Kuyper Kendall, Bo Shinkle and Anson Seibert led the way. ⚾
@_benbybee @Cooper_Kelly2 @AnsonSeibert @KuyperKendall1 @BVSW_BSB

Blue Valley Southwest... · 5/27/22
2022 5A STATE CHAMPIONS!!!!!!

9

Kevin Dempsey @Dempsey_... · 5/27/22 ···
Get to know this kid. Absolute beast mode.
⚾@AnsonSeibert

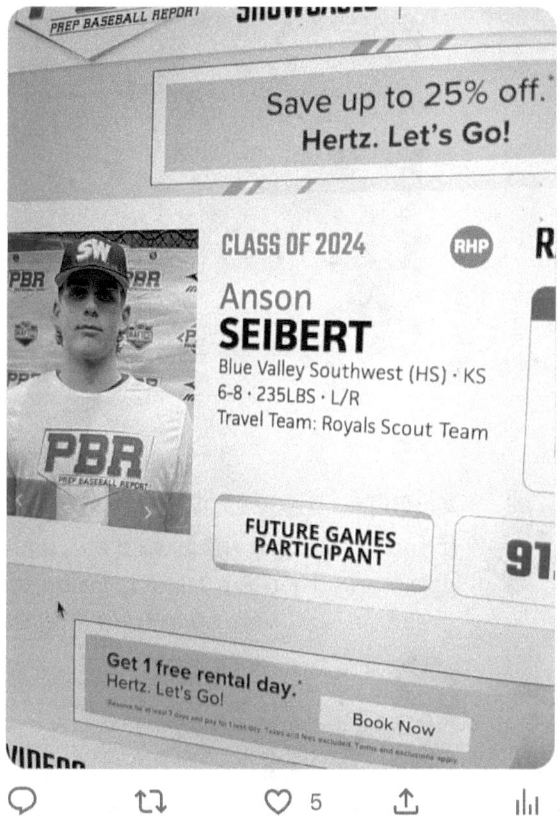

5

Kevin Dempsey @Dempsey_... · 5/27/22 ···

RIP Ray Liotta

2

Kevin Dempsey @Dempsey_P... · 6/3/22 ···

If you are getting ready to play a baseball game and the other team is doing this pregame, you may be in for a long day...

1 8

Kevin Dempsey @Dempsey_P... · 6/3/22 ···
Always nice to witness good team chemistry...⚾ @macnseitzkc @NikolausCrouch @HunterGudde

3 15

Kevin Dempsey @Dempsey_P... · 6/3/22 ···

New Mexico State was 4-11 in WAC conference play. Went 4-0 in their conference tournament. Now playing at Oregon State in the Regional Opening round. Another reminder to never give up!!!! ⚾

1

Kevin Dempsey @Dempsey_P... · 6/4/22 ···

Favorite matchup for today's Regional Round? ⚾

Arkansas v Oklahoma State	**56%**
Florida v Oklahoma	33%
Florida State v Auburn	11%

9 votes · Final results

3

Kevin Dempsey @Dempsey_P... · 6/4/22 ···

Club tournament games should begin at 10am. 8am games are not in the best interest of anyone...

4

Kevin Dempsey @Dempsey_P... · 6/4/22 ···

Who will win the NCAA Baseball Championship? 🏆

Arkansas	19%
Tennessee	**44%**
Stanford	19%
Oregon State	18%

16 votes · Final results

Kevin Dempsey @Dempsey_P... · 6/4/22 ···
Who will win the NCAA Baseball Championship? - Underdog Edition 🏆

New Mexico State	0%
East Carolina	40%
Long Island	0%
Missouri State	**60%**

5 votes · Final results

2

Kevin Dempsey @Dempsey_P... · 6/4/22 ···
If the team you just played is taking a team selfie after the game, you probably had a rough day.... ⚾

12

Kevin Dempsey @Dempsey_P... · 6/4/22 ···

Saw a kid throw a no hitter today. Respect.
@jake_riggin4

1 7

Kevin Dempsey @Dempsey_P... · 6/4/22 ···

Hey PBR Missouri, this kid just threw a no hitter in one of your tournaments today at Creekside. Still unranked. Curveball is legit. Please reconsider Jake Riggin for your top #100 2025's in Missouri. Thank you!
@PBRMissouri @NikolausCrouch
@jake_riggin4

CLASS OF 2025

Jake
RIGGIN

Kevin Dempsey @Dempsey_P... · 6/4/22 ···
I think Robert Moore is ready to break out big time tonight at Oklahoma State in the NCAA Regionals. Go Hogs!
@__robertmoore_ @RazorbackBSB

4

Kevin Dempsey @Dempsey_P... · 6/5/22 ···
Another reminder to never give up, not just on the baseball field, but in the game of life!

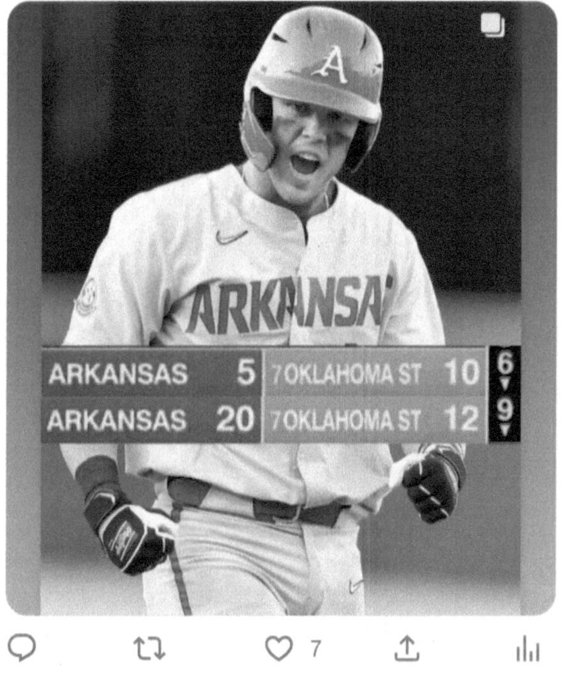

7

Kevin Dempsey @Dempsey_P... · 6/5/22 ···

I love these socks! @Vol_Baseball

5

Kevin Dempsey @Dempsey_P... · 6/6/22 ···
Who will win NCAA D1 Regional Final tonight? 📚 ⚾ @NCAABaseball

Arkansas Razorbacks	33%
Oklahoma State Cowboys	**67%**

3 votes · Final results

2

Kevin Dempsey @Dempsey_P... · 6/6/22 ···
Podcast interview link below about me and the upcoming book called The Republic Baseball League... 📚 ⚾

> **Mike Lindsley** @MikeL... · 6/6/22
> Today's podcast is up. @scooterfink chats about his upcoming fictional novel, his beloved Royals, the state of the game, his son ball hawking at games, Baseball Gods and Music Gods...

2 4

Kevin Dempsey @Dempsey_P... · 6/6/22 ···
TCU Athletic Director made a great decision to retain the rest of the coaching staff after Head Coach Jim Schlossnagle left for Texas A & M. I think Tulane should do the same. Roll wave! @Tulane_AD @GreenWaveBSB

1 6

Kevin Dempsey @Dempsey_P... · 6/6/22 ···

Brewers pitcher Brent Suter is now a published author. Good stuff!! 📚@bruter24

3

Kevin Dempsey @Dempsey_P... · 6/6/22 ···
Not the same pitching staff as last year (Wicklander, Kopps), but this Arkansas team has that special something. ⚾
@RazorbackBSB @__robertmoore_

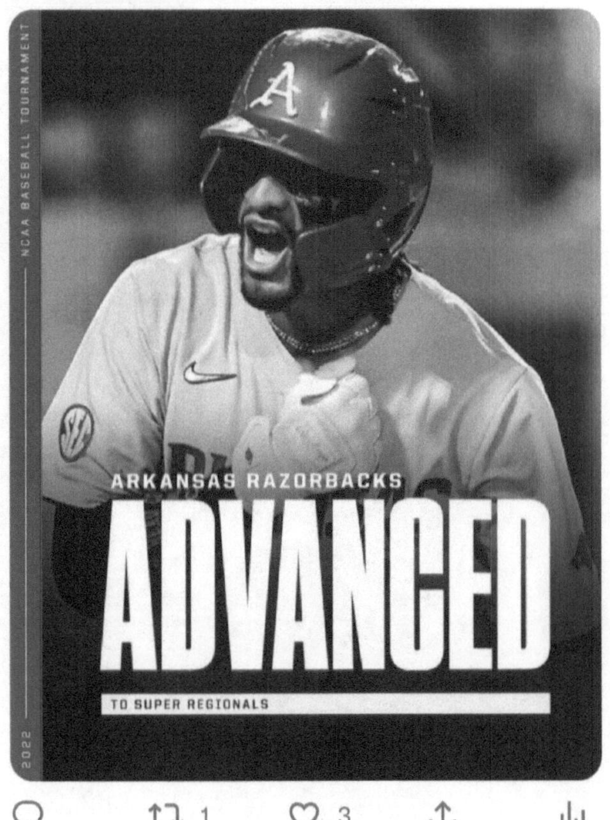

1 3

Kevin Dempsey @Dempsey_P... · 6/6/22 ···

I really like what Skip Johnson and his staff (Overcash, Willits, Bonneau) is doing over there in Norman, Oklahoma.

Oklahoma Baseball · 6/6/22

LET'S GOOOOOOOOOOOOO!

#Boomer

2 18

Kevin Dempsey @Dempsey_P... · 6/6/22 ···
Oklahoma Freshman Jackson Nicklaus, another Kansas City kid, is one to watch.. @j_nick5 @OU_Baseball

Oklahoma Baseball · 6/6/22
Nicklaus adds another!

📺 ESPNNEWS

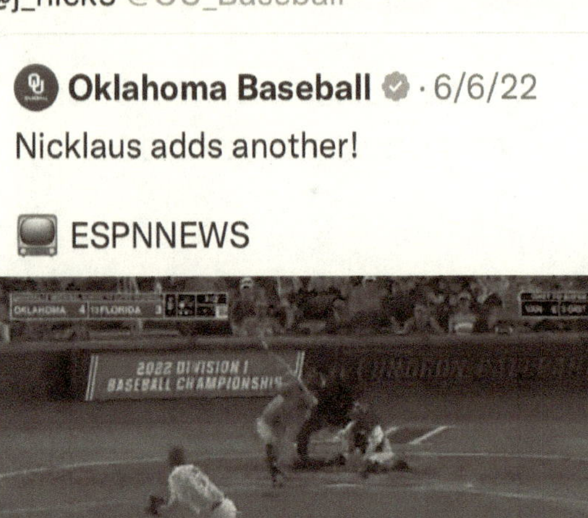

9

Kevin Dempsey @Dempsey_P... · 6/7/22 ···
Heartbreaking loss to Stanford tonight in the NCAA Regionals, but Texas State was great all season and they are going to be good for years to come. So many good college baseball programs in Texas. Baylor job open, big opportunity. 📚⚾

5

Kevin Dempsey @Dempsey_P... · 6/7/22 ···
And so it begins....⚾

4

Kevin Dempsey @Dempsey_P... · 6/7/22 ···
Congratulations to Tulane's new baseball head coach Jay Uhlman! Roll wave!
@Tulane_AD @jezk1010

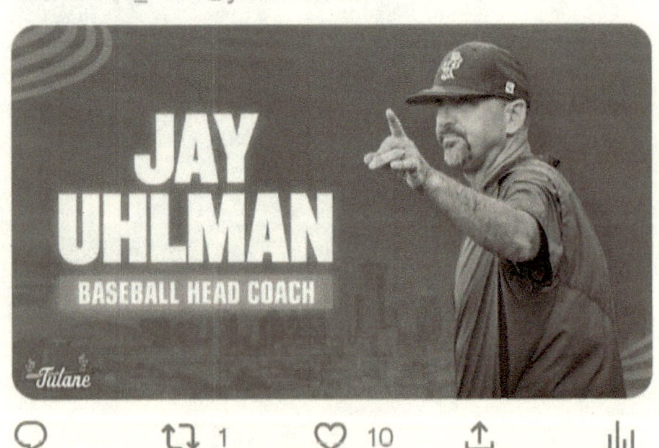

1 10

Kevin Dempsey @Dempsey_P... · 6/8/22 ···

Many sports critics think that Manfred is slowing killing the game of baseball, but I am grateful for guys like Zack Hample who are trying to save it! ⚾ @zack_hample

5

Kevin Dempsey @Dempsey_P... · 6/9/22 ···
Sports reporters who reference the work of the baseball gods have my respect.
@JeffPassan @scooterfink

2

Kevin Dempsey @Dempsey_P... · 6/9/22 ···
Always adding to my baseball bucket list...
⚾

3

Kevin Dempsey @Dempsey_P... · 6/9/22 ···

Coaches, like school teachers come and go, but, like teachers, good coaches can have a positive impact on a player that can last forever! 📚

4 46

Kevin Dempsey @Dempsey_P... · 6/9/22 ···

Baseball coaches wearing knickers? Yes indeed! More of that please. ⚾

4

Kevin Dempsey @Dempsey_... · 6/10/22 ···

The sound of a well hit baseball with a wood bat is beautiful. Shout out to Perfect Game for hosting wood bat only tournaments. @PerfectGameUSA @PG_Tourney

8

Kevin Dempsey @Dempsey_... · 6/12/22 ···

Witnessed a coach talking to his runner on third base during a pitching change. Tie game. Bottom of the 6th with no time left. Before first pitch, walk off stolen base to win the game. Cheap trick or good coaching? 🤷

Kevin Dempsey @Dempsey_... · 6/12/22 ···

Pop quiz: How many times did Jackie Robinson steal home?........19!

4

Kevin Dempsey @Dempsey_... · 6/13/22 ···

Uncanny! ⚡

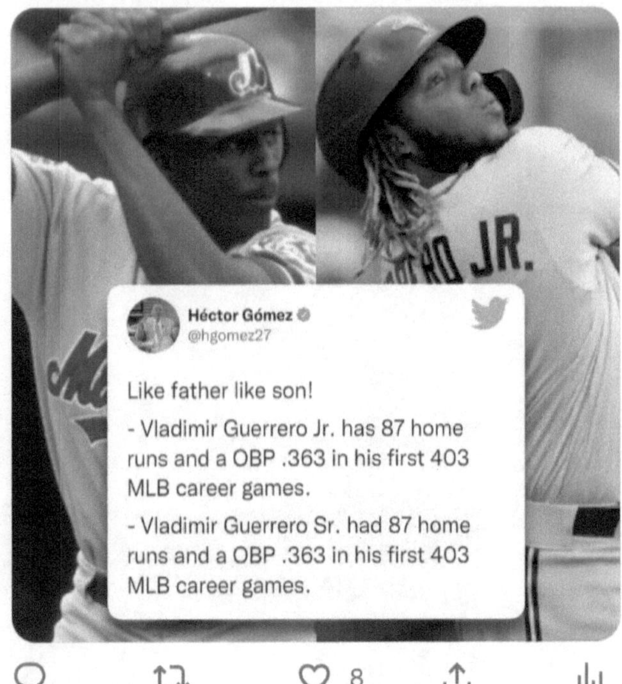

8

Kevin Dempsey @Dempsey_.... · 6/13/22 ···
A pitcher who politely asks his coach with 2 outs and the bases loaded to stay in the game, has my respect. No matter the outcome. I want that kid on my team.
@andersonkaemmer @HunterGudde @Sutti_25 @NikolausCrouch

2 12

Kevin Dempsey @Dempsey_.... · 6/14/2
Who will win the College World Series?

Arkansas

Oklahoma

Stanford

Texas A & M

12 votes · Final results

1

Kevin Dempsey @Dempsey_... · 6/14/22 ···

Being a little league umpire is a thankless job...

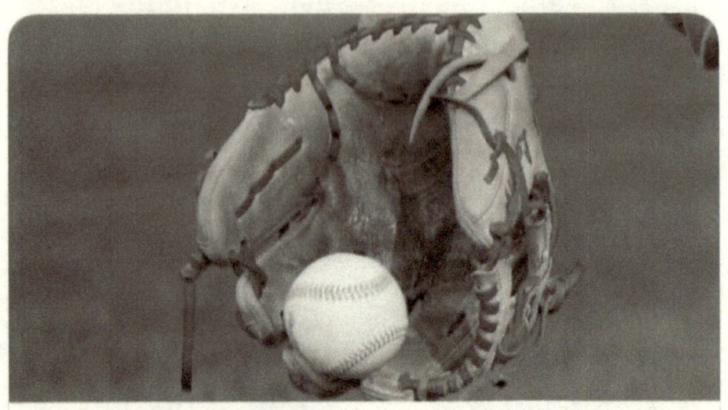

cbssports.com

Youth baseball coach breaks 72-year-old umpire's jaw with 'sucker punch' during...

2 2

Kevin Dempsey @Dempsey_... · 6/15/22 ···
My favorite books to read are about economics, politics, the capital markets, spirituality and baseball📚⚾

6

Kevin Dempsey @Dempsey_... · 6/15/22 ···
Protect the plate! If you are in a 2-strike count, swing that bat! You may foul it off, you may put the ball in play, but good things can happen! @fink_14

88 views

4

Kevin Dempsey @Dempsey_... · 6/15/22 ···
Kansas finished in last place in the Big 12 baseball standings in 2022. I see a program turnaround on the horizon 🌅

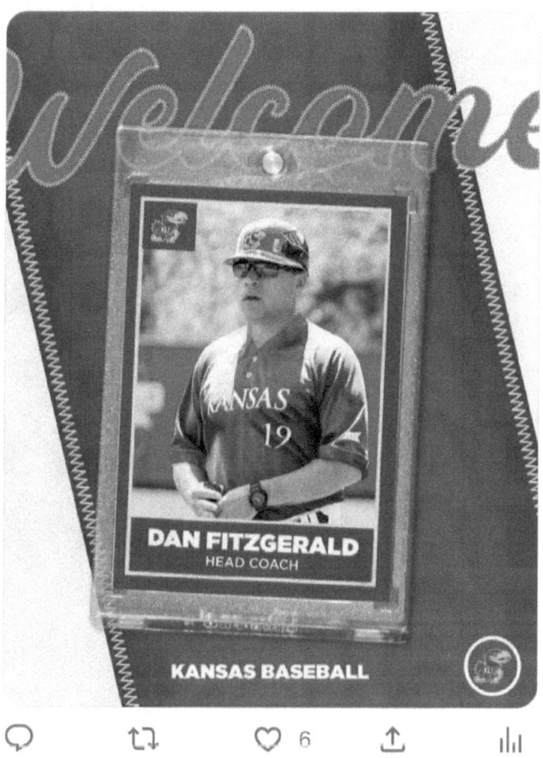

6

Kevin Dempsey @Dempsey_... · 6/15/22 ···
I am a big supporter of dugout rituals, but a pimp coat after a home run? 🤷
@Vol_Baseball @NCAABaseball

2

Kevin Dempsey @Dempsey_... · 6/16/22 ···
This kid Ashton Nance is the real deal. 2025, but he's playing up. 14 years old! @ashton_nance @PBRMissouri

Andy Urban PBR @PbrU... · 6/16/22

2025 1B Ashton Nance (Blue Springs South HS, MO) stays back and uses his 6'3, 210-pound frame to drive this ball up the middle with authority for @macnseitzkc. Very interesting follow. @PBRTournaments @PBRMissouri #CreeksideSummerChampionship

7

Kevin Dempsey @Dempsey_... · 6/16/22 ···

The George Washington University ending use of 'Colonials' nickname...

2

Kevin Dempsey @Dempsey_... · 6/17/22 ···

I don't love the new look of the Big 12 or the American Conference, but I love the fact that schools have the liberty to move around. Free market capitalism!

5

Kevin Dempsey @Dempsey_... · 6/17/22 ···

First of all, remember the name Cooper Kelly. Incoming short stop/third baseman at Kansas. The dude is clutch. Second, I liked the home run ritual at the end of the video. Cute. ⚡ @Cooper_Kelly2

Vermont Lake Monst... · 6/16/22

We see you @Cooper_Kelly2 💪

#GOMonsters #MonsterHR
twitter.com/VTLakeMonsters...

9

Kevin Dempsey @Dempsey_... · 6/17/22 ···

Some guys are really into cars, I'm really into economics, politics, and baseball jerseys.

@OU_Baseball

6

Kevin Dempsey @Dempsey_... · 6/17/22 ···
Texas A&M Head Coach Jim Schlossnagle. I've met the man and watched him coach. Big fan. Amazing he's already back in Omaha! @CoachSchloss @NCAABaseball

3

Kevin Dempsey @Dempsey_... · 6/18/22 ···
Unwritten Rule of Baseball: Whatever time your coach tells you to be there, be there 15 minutes earlier...

6

Kevin Dempsey @Dempsey_... · 6/18/22 ···

There is a old saying that goes like this: “Offense sells tickets, but defense wins championships” ⚡ @fink_14

Kevin Dempsey @Dempsey_... · 6/18/22 ···
Important Reminder: Never talk about a no hitter, during a no-hitter. ⚡

4

Kevin Dempsey @Dempsey_... · 6/18/22 ···
Ok, fine. I can think of one good thing about 8am baseball games in the summer. The weather.

3

Kevin Dempsey @Dempsey_... · 6/20/22 ···
Big fan of pitcher Ben Bybee. I like his curveball and his fastball, but what impresses me the most about this mlb draft prospect is that he's a nice person. Scouts have a chart for that? @_benbybee @MLB @DaytonMoore22

Kevin Bybee @KevinByb... · 6/20/22
11 weeks after his first high school pitching start ever (thanks to COVID year and TJ surgery), @_benbybee got to do his thing at the MLB Combine. Special shout out to @Premier_BB_KC @TMISportsMed @JYoder_PTKC @tykin27 #tjsuccess
Show this thread

Kevin Dempsey @Dempsey_... · 6/22/22 ···
Been watching the College World Series all week on television. Excited to watch two games today from the stands. ⚡ @PerezEd @espn

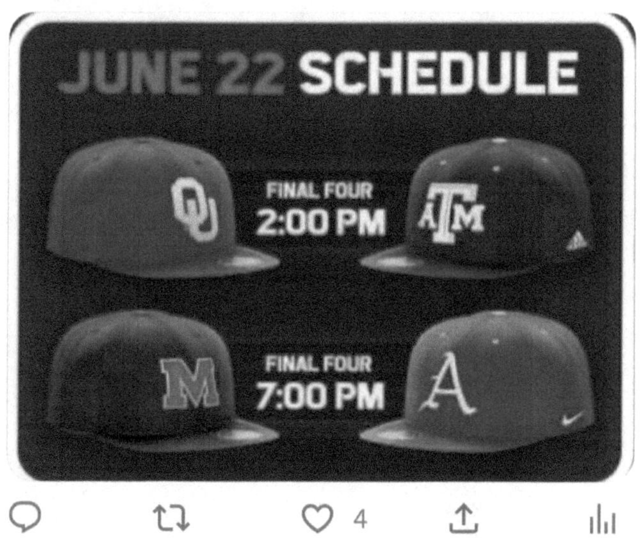

4

Kevin Dempsey @Dempsey_... · 6/22/22 ···

She's a beauty... ⚡ @NCAABaseball

13

Kevin Dempsey @Dempsey_... · 6/22/22 ···
Congrats to Robert Moore!

5

Kevin Dempsey @Dempsey_... · 6/22/22 ···

Texas A&M fans did not bring their bubble ritual to Omaha with them. Big mistake! @AggieBaseball #MCWS

2

Kevin Dempsey @Dempsey_... · 6/22/22 ···
Just another kid from Kansas hitting a home run in the College World Series.
@RazorbackBSB @brady_slavens

Arkansas Baseball · 6/22/22

You almost never see anyone go to dead center at this ballpark...

Except if it's @brady_slavens

6

Kevin Dempsey @Dempsey_... · 6/22/22 ···

Texas A&M's baseball team does not utilize bat boys. They have the Diamond Darlings.

@aggiediamonds

3

Kevin Dempsey @Dempsey_... · 6/22/22 ···
Good karma... ⚡ @j_nick5

134 views

3

Kevin Dempsey @Dempsey_... · 6/23/22 ···
There are 299 Division 1 baseball teams. Only 8 get to play in the College World Series. Just making it to Omaha is remarkable. I love this end of season speech by Coach Van Horn!

Arkansas Baseball · 6/23/22
Proud to be an Arkansas Razorback

8

Kevin Dempsey @Dempsey_... · 6/24/22 ···
"If you build it, he will come." - The Field of Dreams

199 views

8

Kevin Dempsey @Dempsey_... · 6/24/22 ···

"They'll arrive at your door as innocent as children, longing for the past. Of course, we won't mind if you look around, you'll say. It's only $20 per person." - Terrence Mann (Field of Dreams)

Kevin Dempsey @Dempsey_P... · 7/2/22 ···

The Journey is the Destination...

6

Kevin Dempsey @Dempsey_P... · 7/2/22 ···

I think "The Big 10 Conference" needs a name change...

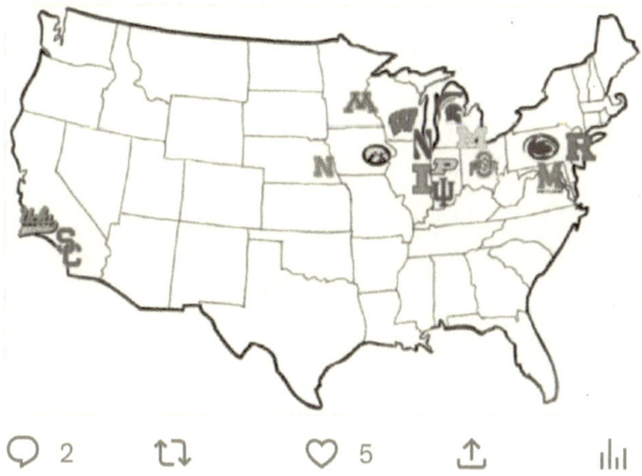

2 5

Kevin Dempsey @Dempsey_P... · 7/3/22 ···

Powder blue baseball uniforms? YES

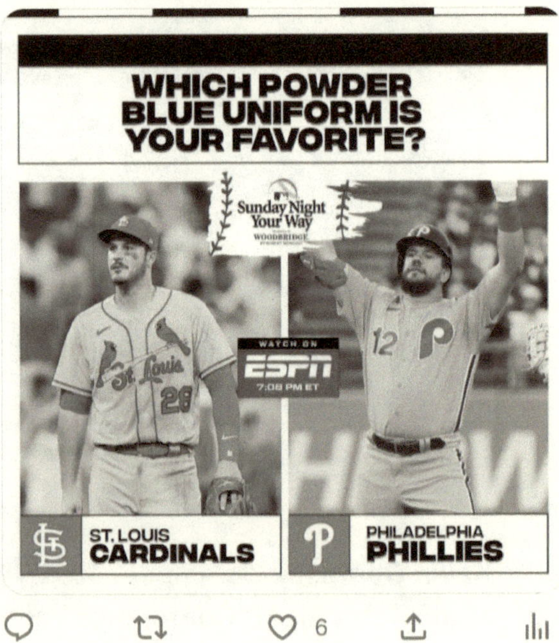

6

Kevin Dempsey @Dempsey_P... · 7/6/22 ···
As a college professor, who happens to love college baseball, I say kudos to you, Tulane University, well done. Nice to see! Roll wave! 🌊📚⚡ @jezk1010

Tulane Baseball @Gree... · 7/5/22
Some of  are on campus for summer classes.

Future is bright Uptown 😎

1 1 23

Kevin Dempsey @Dempsey_P... · 7/6/22 ···

With conferences in such disarray at the moment, I think NCAA athletic directors will eventually come around to the idea that a "Promotion and Relegation" model is the best option. One big league, lots of divisions and a few schools moving up and down after each season. ⚡ @ncaa

2

Kevin Dempsey @Dempsey_P... · 7/6/22 ···

One more thing @ncaa, when you merge all the D1 school together into one big promotion & relegation league system like European Football, include JUCO's, D2 and D3 programs! ⚡ @NCAA @NCAABaseball @NJCAA

1 2

Kevin Dempsey @Dempsey_P... · 7/7/22 ···

The World Baseball Classic is good for humanity... ⚡

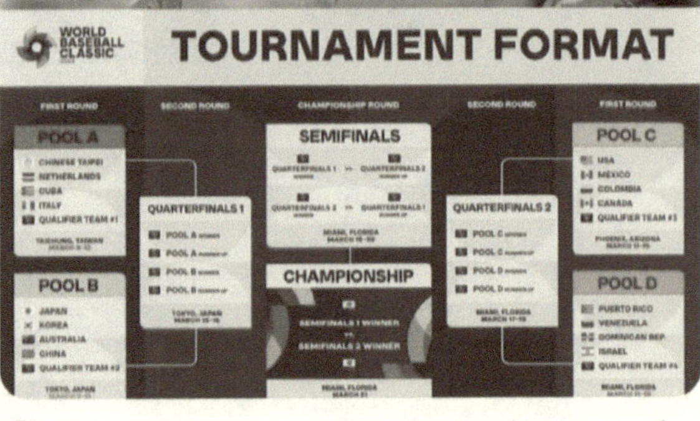

2 9

Kevin Dempsey @Dempsey_P... · 7/7/22 ···
USC Baseball just got themselves an absolute gem of a coach. The kind of coach that is willing to stand up for his other coaches and defend them! Best of luck Coach Jewett! ⚡ @TJewett50 @jezk1010 @AdamCoreTU @fink_14

USC Baseball @USC_B... · 7/7/22
The staff is starting to take shape! Please welcome Assistant Coach Travis Jewett to the TrojanFamily! 🙌⚾✌
Show this thread

Kevin Dempsey @Dempsey_P... · 7/8/22 ···

This sign post has got it backwards, it's capitalism to the right and socialism, to the left...

3

Kevin Dempsey @Dempsey_P... · 7/8/22 ···

Knickers high up as shorts? I think that's taking things a bit too far

1 5

Kevin Dempsey @Dempsey_P... · 7/8/22 ···
MLB draft next week. Predicting that Arkansas second baseman Robert "Bobby" Moore will get drafted, but maybe not by the Kansas City Royals, but perhaps by the Atlanta Braves! @__robertmoore_ @DaytonMoore22

4

Kevin Dempsey @Dempsey_P... · 7/8/22 ···

Knickers above the knee has become a baseball fashion trend...

4

Kevin Dempsey @Dempsey_... · 7/12/22 ···
This video game needs a comeback ⚡ @EASPORTS @NCAABaseball

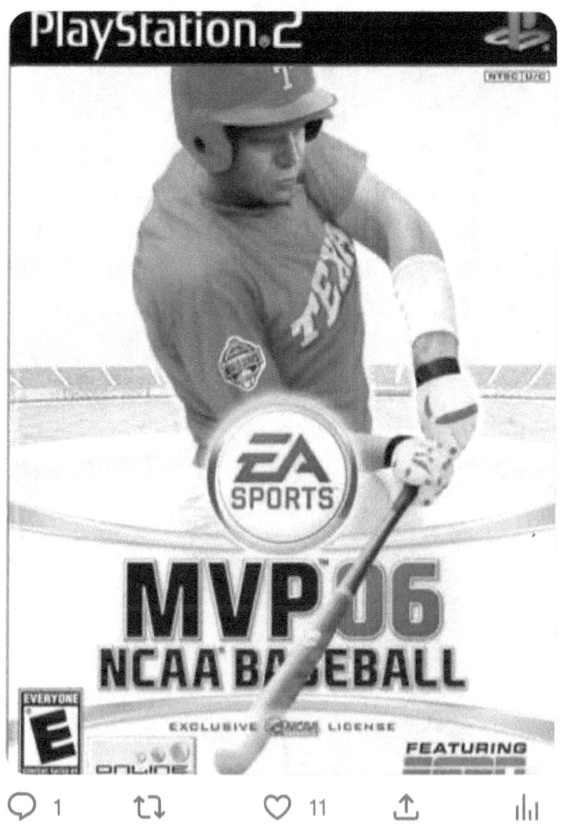

1 11

Kevin Dempsey @Dempsey_... · 7/13/22 ···
Huge upside for Brandon Hill. Best part, he's a nice person

Sean Smith @_SeanSmit... · 7/12/22

'25 OF Brandon Hill (@RoyalsScoutTeam) cruises into second with an easy double. Smooth and athletic swing with a lot of juice. Fluid rhythm in all movements with more to come as he continues to mature.

@PBRMissouri @ShooterHunt
#PBR15uNat

4

Kevin Dempsey @Dempsey_... · 7/13/22 ···

J.T. Realmuto and all those Kansas City Royals, you have my respect.

97.1 The Ticket · 21h ··· X

Defiant J.T. Realmuto says vaccine 'not worth it': 'I'm not going to let Canada tell me what to put in my body'

601 25 Shares

1 9

Kevin Dempsey @Dempsey_P... · 7/17/22 ···
Congrats to Robert Moore!

4

Kevin Dempsey @Dempsey_P... · 7/17/22 ···
High School and College baseball players should be considered free agents and be able to sign with any professional team they want...

1 7

Kevin Dempsey @Dempsey_... · 7/19/22 ···

It costs nothing to be a nice person ⚡

1 10

Kevin Dempsey @Dempsey_... · 7/25/22 ···

OOTP Baseball 23 ⚡ 🎮

 **Elon Musk** @elonmusk · 7/25/22

What video games have you enjoyed most over past year or two?

2

Kevin Dempsey @Dempsey_... · 7/23/22 ···

I am looking forward to the day when baseball fans all across the country are reading the fictional novel about Professor Dempsey and The Republic Baseball League... @RBL___

2 12

Kevin Dempsey @Dempsey_... · 7/26/22

Baseball Economy update...

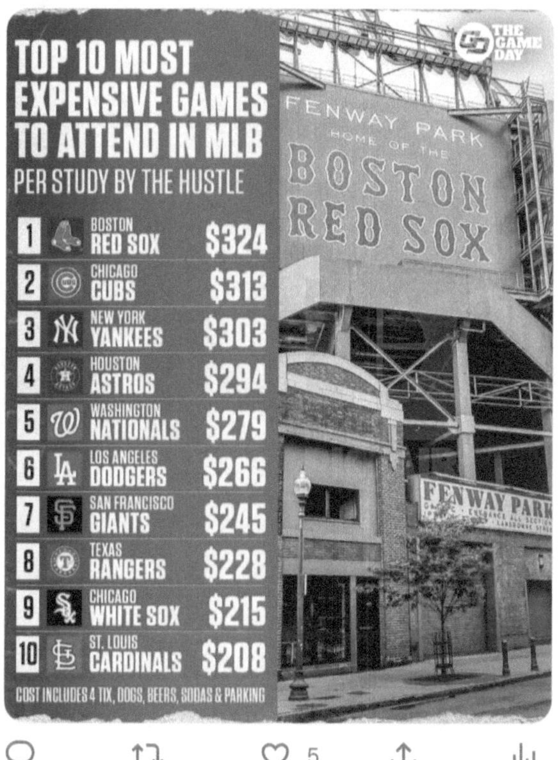

5

Kevin Dempsey @Dempsey_... · 7/26/22 ···

The rising cost to attend a MLB game is one of the big reasons game attendance has declined in recent years...

7

Kevin Dempsey @Dempsey_... · 7/27/22 ···
It's not a coincidence that good things happen to baseball players with good karma... ⚡ @Jalenbattles2

Kevin Dempsey @Dempsey_P... · 8/6/22 ···

The Savannah Bananas uniforms are looking good! ⚡ @TheSavBananas

4

Kevin Dempsey @Dempsey_P... · 8/8/22

Must be surreal to see yourself in MLB The Show... @MLBTheShow @Ivanhoe19721 @__robertmoore_

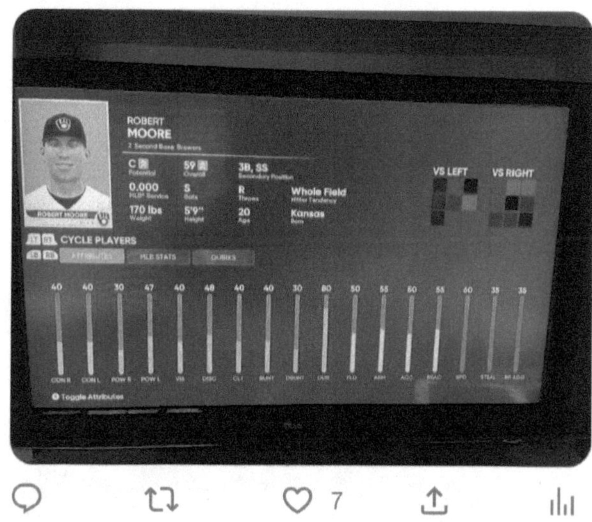

7

Kevin Dempsey @Dempsey_... · 8/10/22 ···
I'd replace Major League 2 with The Natural, but otherwise, well done Ben Verlander!
@BenVerlander

7

Kevin Dempsey @Dempsey_... · 8/21/22 ···

I concur...

1 5

Kevin Dempsey @Dempsey_... · 8/21/22 ···

Baseball Economics update...

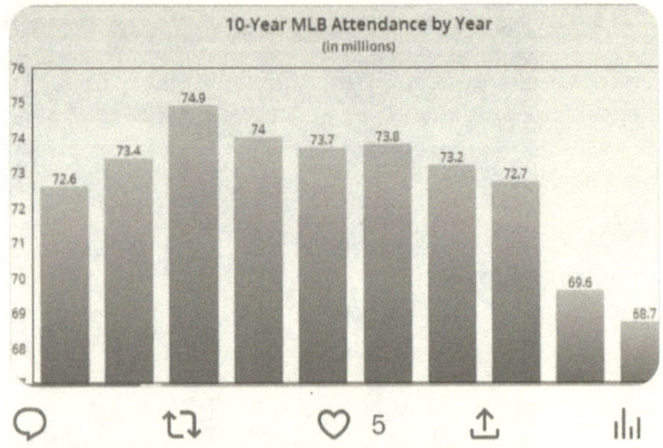

5

Kevin Dempsey @Dempsey_... · 8/21/22 ···

Great story! Also great to have a college degree so you have a Plan B

17

Kevin Dempsey @Dempsey_... · 8/23/22 ···
The George Washington Colonials have an adorable baseball stadium...

1 9

Kevin Dempsey @Dempsey_... · 8/23/22 ···

I'd like to see a chart of minor league baseball teams and their profitability during recessions... ⚾💵⚡

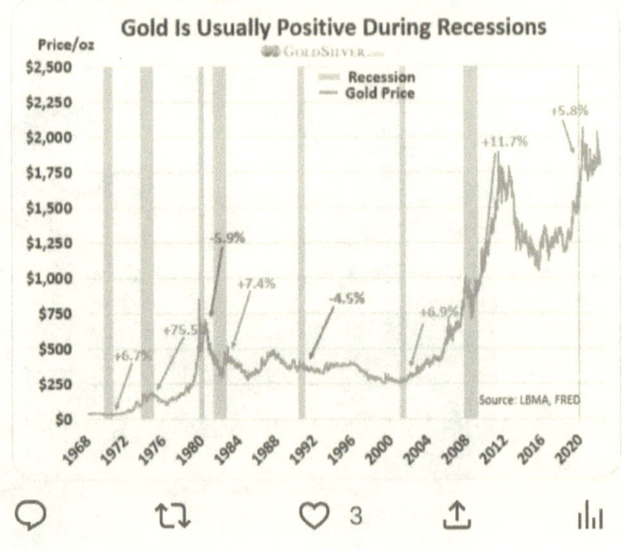

3

Kevin Dempsey @Dempsey_... · 8/23/22 ···
Shout out to all the universities that offer a major in Political Economy...

5

Kevin Dempsey @Dempsey_... · 8/24/22 ···

I'd like to do a summer lecture series called "The Metaphysics of Baseball" and speak at universities all over the country. Visit a minor league ballpark in every city I visit...

7

Kevin Dempsey @Dempsey_... · 9/11/22 ···

Haymaker Park, home to the University of Nebraska and the Lincoln Saltdogs is awesome! @Husker_Baseball @lincolnsaltdogs @RBL___

218 views

9

Kevin Dempsey @Dempsey_... · 9/21/22 ···

At times like this, I need to remember that baseball is a business...

Jeff Passan @JeffPas... · 9/21/22

The Kansas City Royals fired president of baseball operations Dayton Moore, their longtime top baseball executive and the architect of their 2015 World Series championship.

Show this thread

4

Kevin Dempsey @Dempsey_... · 9/21/22 ···

An idea can be manifested into reality...

ign.com

Ted Lasso and AFC Richmond Officially Announced for FIFA 23 - IGN

4

Kevin Dempsey @Dempsey_... · 9/22/22 ···

Yordano Ventura passed away in 2017 in a tragic car accident. He would only be 31 years old today. It was Dayton Moore who signed this once in a generation pitcher. The Royals would have been a wild card potential team every season if we still had him RIP#30 @Royals @goldbergkc

1 11

Kevin Dempsey @Dempsey_... · 9/22/22 ···

Attention middle school and high school baseball players: It's the off-season, focus on getting good grades right now, but also keep working hard in the gym to become the best version of you in 2023! ⚡ @fink_14

306 views

 1  8

Kevin Dempsey @Dempsey_... · 9/24/22 ···

reason.com

Declining faith in both capitalism and socialism leaves...what?

3

Kevin Dempsey @Dempsey_... · 9/25/22 ···

The Tequila Sunrise....

4

Kevin Dempsey @Dempsey_... · 9/26/22 ···

Daily Reminder: Freedom, Liberty & Capitalism is good. Tyranny, authoritarianism, communism and socialism is bad....

9

Kevin Dempsey @Dempsey_... · 9/26/22 ···

High schools should stop teaching Algebra and replace it with class about Personal Finance...

8

Kevin Dempsey @Dempsey_... · 10/1/22 ···
My favorite hobby...

7

Kevin Dempsey @Dempsey_... · 10/1/22 ···

See you tomorrow Eck Stadium...

9

Kevin Dempsey @Dempsey_... · 10/2/22 ···

It's time to bring back the Wichita State football program! @TedLasso @FootballGods44 @GoShockersBSB

321 views

1 10

Kevin Dempsey @Dempsey_... · 10/7/22 ···

On a 3-2 count, protect the plate!

11

Kevin Dempsey @Dempsey_... · 10/7/22 ···

Been having a recurring dream lately where I own my own pro baseball team in The Republic Baseball League and we build a ballpark on our family farm outside of Wichita, KS... ⚡ @RBL___ 🇺🇸⚾

1 5

Kevin Dempsey @Dempsey_... · 10/11/22 ···
Attention High School baseball players that don't play football: Consider playing in a once a week fall ball rec league with your friends just for the love of the game. No coaches, sandlot style. And make sure to include the incoming freshman! @fink_14

277 views

1 1 6

Kevin Dempsey @Dempsey... · 10/12/22 ···

Playing sports video games is fun, it stimulates the mind. But if you want to stimulate your mind and fuel your soul, read books... ⚡

288 views

1 6

Kevin Dempsey @Dempsey... · 10/14/22 ···
Every town needs their own baseball card store...

1 9

Kevin Dempsey @Dempsey... · 10/15/22 ···

Trading baseball cards is fun...

1 8

Kevin Dempsey @Dempsey... · 10/16/22 ···

I'm always looking for a gem...

4

Kevin Dempsey @Dempsey_... · 10/17/22 ···
Saw a 2025 baseball player hitting 100 mph off a pitching machine today with ease. Beautiful, powerful swing. Mark my words, this kid is getting drafted. His name is Colton Sims... @MLB @BCbaseballtoday @theColtonSims

3 39

Kevin Dempsey @Dempsey... · 10/22/22 ···
I think I am going to hang this flag on the wall in my lecture hall. "Don't Tread On Me" is an expression of freedom and Liberty...

8

Kevin Dempsey @Dempsey... · 10/23/22 ···

Clubhouses have changed a lot since I played college ball at Wichita State in the 1980's. Kansas State, your baseball facilities are looking good! Best of luck to you guys in 2023! @KStateBSB

16

Kevin Dempsey @Dempsey... · 10/23/22 ···
Astrology Update: Solar Eclipse this Tuesday, October 25, 2022...

6

Kevin Dempsey @Dempsey... · 10/23/22 ···

I'd like to wish a get well soon to Wichita State head baseball coach Eric Wedge. I hope you are back at practice soon... @GoShockersBSB @CoachEricWedge

16

Kevin Dempsey @Dempsey... · 10/31/22 ···

Astrology Update...

The 1st ever Election Day Blood Moon lunar eclipse is coming on Nov. 8

By Joe Rao published 4 days ago

This will be the second and final lunar eclipse of 2022.

A photograph of a total lunar eclipse in Canta, east of Lima on May 15, 2022. (Image credit: ERNESTO BENAVIDES/AFP via Getty Images)

 4

Kevin Dempsey @Dempsey... · 10/31/22 ···

I really enjoyed watching KU baseball practice this week. Players showed up to the clubhouse in Halloween costumes. Good for team chemistry! 🎃 @Cooper_Kelly2

193 views

9

Kevin Dempsey @Dempsey_... · 11/3/22 ···
PSP3 Strength Training and Conditioning in Kansas City is the best in the biz. Shout out to Nate Hemphill and Derek Gordon...
@DerekGordon05 @PSP3nation

 **Nate Fink 2025** @fink_14 · 11/3/22

355 for 2 RPE9

@PSP3nation
@bvnbaseball1
@TyKav12
@RitchieGregg
@CJONeill511

1 10

Kevin Dempsey @Dempsey_... · 11/4/22 ···

My college students know how much I admire baseball jerseys. Tulane's baseball jersey logo pays homage to the former minor league New Orleans Pelicans and the St. Louis Cardinals. The Green Wave have the best portfolio of baseball uniforms in the NCAA... ⚡ @jezk1010 @Coach_Izz5

Tulane Baseball @Gre... · 11/4/22

Jerseys so beautiful, they should be celebrated everyday.

#RollWave 🌊 ⚾ | #NationalJerseyDay

14

Kevin Dempsey @Dempsey_... · 11/10/22 ···
The Baseball Gods love this kid...
@__robertmoore_ @Brewers

Brisbane Bandits @B... · 11/10/22
ANOTHER ONE 💥 Robert Moore goes deep for his 2nd home-run of the night!!

Score: Brisbane 6 - Auckland 0

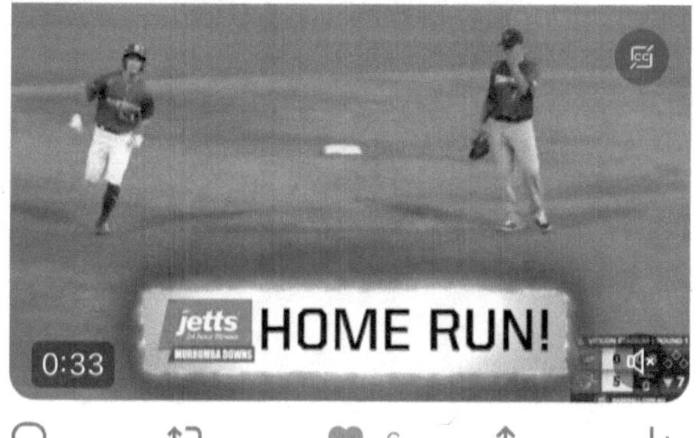

6

Kevin Dempsey @Dempsey_... · 11/8/22 ···

It's Election Day! It does not matter to me if you are a Democrat, Republican, Green Party or Libertarian, but it does matter to me that you don't take your right to vote for granted... 🇺🇸

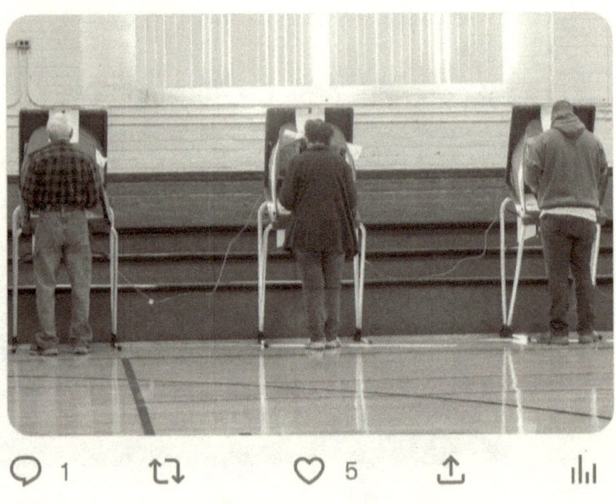

1 5

Kevin Dempsey @Dempsey_... · 11/8/22 ···
I'm a baseball guy, but I do love my Kansas City Chiefs... ⚡ @Chiefs

7

Kevin Dempsey @Dempsey_... · 11/13/22 ···

What can I say, I love it when my Wichita State Shockers sign kids from my neck of the woods. Last year Devon Wasserman, this year, it's Mason Pangborn! Congrats Mason Pangborn! Also, a tip of the hat to the coaches at Building Champions for another D1 commitment! ⚡ @mpangborn5

Building Champions @... · 11/13/22

Congrats to @mpangborn5 on his commitment to @GoShockersBSB. Big time SS with plus tools. Has a chance to be a difference maker at the next level. High character as well. Happy for the entire Pangborn family. #Committed #BCbaseball #baseball @PBRKansas @homefieldkc @Drew_Olla

1 10

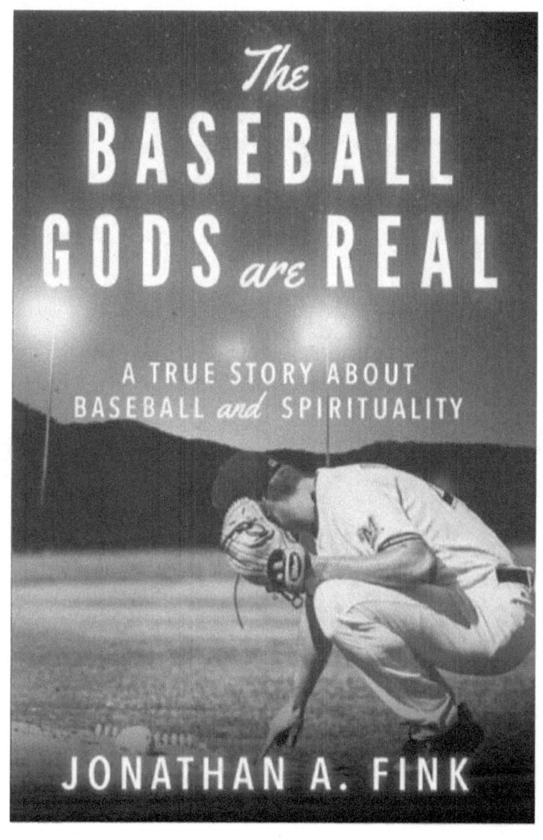
The
BASEBALL
GODS are REAL
A TRUE STORY ABOUT
BASEBALL and SPIRITUALITY
JONATHAN A. FINK

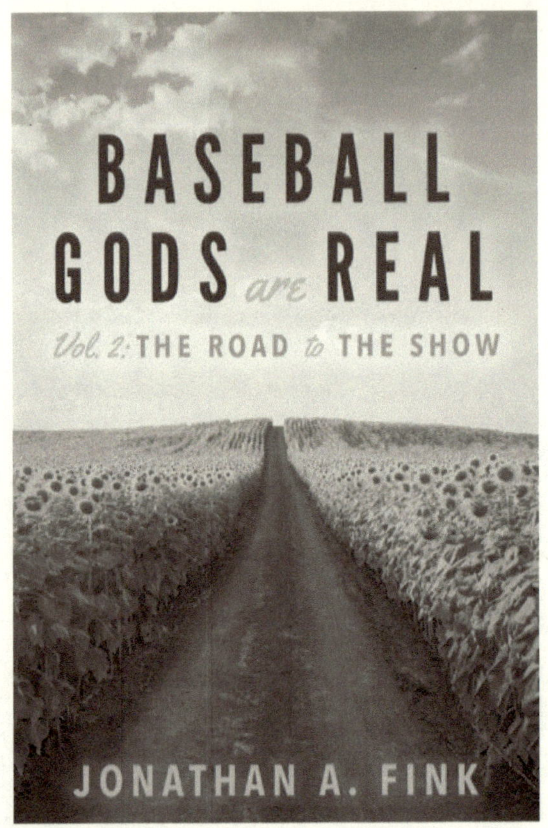
BASEBALL
GODS are REAL
Vol. 2: THE ROAD to THE SHOW
JONATHAN A. FINK

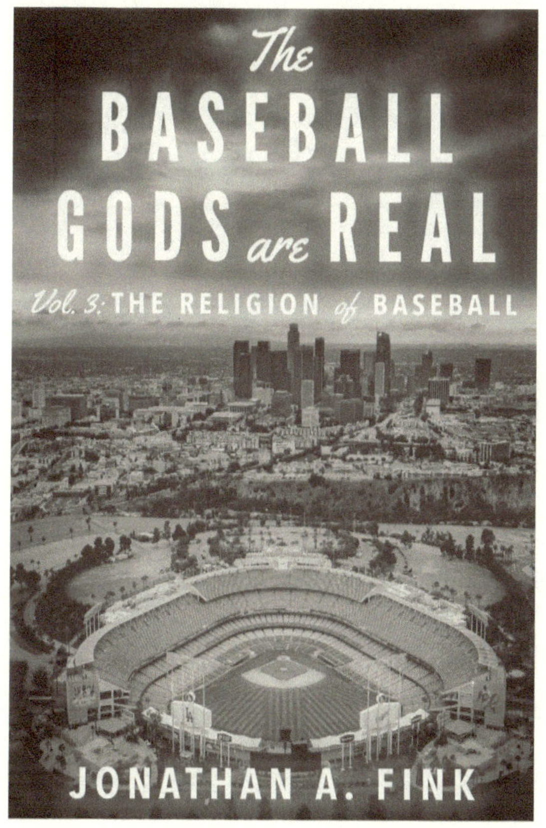
The
BASEBALL
GODS are REAL
Vol. 3: THE RELIGION of BASEBALL
JONATHAN A. FINK

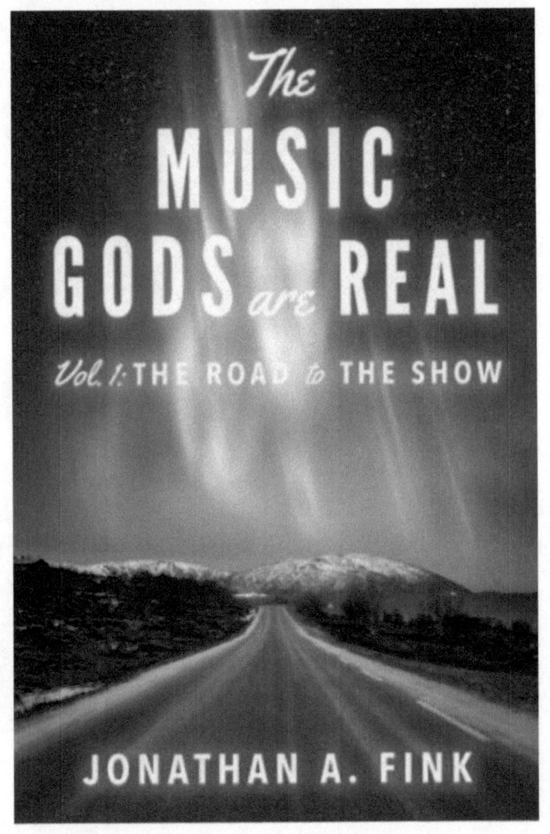
The
MUSIC
GODS are REAL
Vol. 1: THE ROAD to THE SHOW
JONATHAN A. FINK

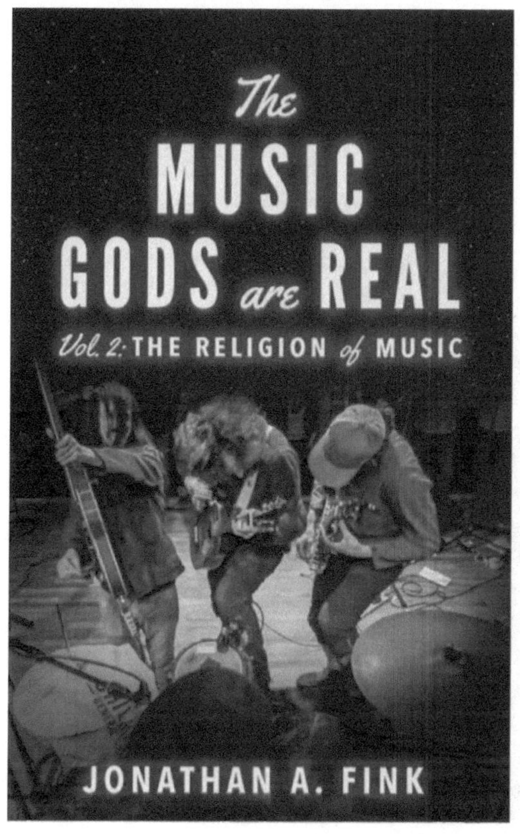
The
MUSIC
GODS are REAL
Vol. 2: THE RELIGION of MUSIC
JONATHAN A. FINK

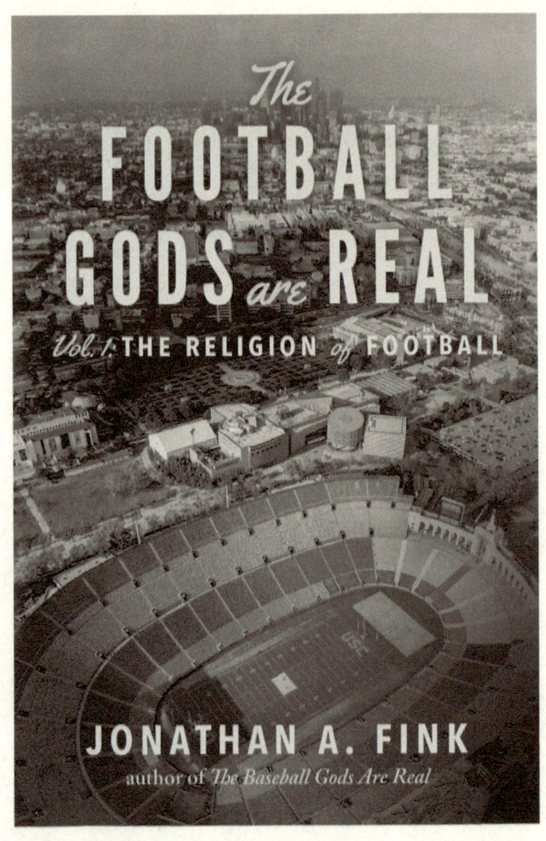
The
FOOTBALL
GODS are REAL
Vol. 1: THE RELIGION of FOOTBALL
JONATHAN A. FINK
author of The Baseball Gods Are Real

www.ingramcontent.com/pod-product-compliance
Lightning Source LLC
LaVergne TN
LVHW091300150826
845673LV00006B/1490

* 9 7 9 8 2 1 8 1 6 2 3 3 7 *